GHOST HASTE

HAUNTED EVERLY AFTER MYSTERIES
BOOK FOUR

REGINA WELLING
ERIN LYNN

Willow Hill
BOOKS

CONTENTS

GHOST HASTE

Bundled in my puffy winter coat and boots over pajamas and a bathrobe, a cup of coffee warming my fingers, I stood on my back porch, watching the dogs romping in the snow and trying to tune out Amber's incessant chatter.

Just my luck, I had to be haunted by a morning ghost.

"It's gonna be a chilly one today. I checked in at the station, and there's a cold front moving in ahead of the big storm. Temps will start to fall around noon, and by the time the ball drops at midnight, we're looking at negative double digits."

It was no shock that the woman had made a career out of talking in front of cameras since, even in death, she couldn't be quiet. I'd have given almost anything for her to settle into a ghostly, atmospheric moan. But no, Amber's mouth only had two speeds: on and off.

She only ever used one of them.

"There was an accident at the grocery store this morning," she continued, fluttering her hands. "Hardly even rated as a fender-bender since no one was hurt, but that Bess Tate sure has a mouth on her. She slid right into the back of a pickup truck, and then yelled at the driver for not getting out of her way fast enough."

At the crack of dawn, with only half a cup of freshly-microwaved, slightly nasty leftover coffee in me, I really didn't care—which said more about my state of alertness than my disregard for those around me. I liked Bess Tate just fine, when I was awake anyway, and would be glad she hadn't been hurt when I fully reached that state. I had no trouble, however, picturing a scenario where she harassed some poor, unfortunate truck owner.

I mumbled something Amber took to be an interested sound because she continued with the story. "He said she was a menace on the road, but she gave it right back. By the time she was done with him, he'd agreed to pay to have a tiny scratch buffed out of her hood, and to bring her a dozen eggs a week for the next two months."

She described the incident in far more detail than my brain could follow, so I tried to tune her out.

December thirty-first.

Wasn't the cusp of the new year supposed to be a pivotal moment? Isn't that why people get so invested in making resolutions?

"Amber." It was time to test one of mine and ask for things I wanted. "Stop talking." Technically, I wasn't asking. "It's not even seven o'clock in the morning. It's barely light out yet, and we both know you woke up the dogs just to get me out of bed. Did dying somehow erase your sense of decency or ability to tell time?"

"Well, excuuuuse me," she said, crossing her arms and scowling.

I couldn't decide if Amber annoyed me in the morning because she was pert and perky or because when I'd been her age—a whopping three years earlier—I, too, had bounced out of bed ready to take on the day.

"I thought you'd want to hear the morning news. It's not like anything interesting happens in this pitiful excuse for a town most of the time, anyway. I'm bored to death."

Boredom hadn't been what killed Amber Hale; she'd died at the hands of a jealous colleague, and then somehow become my problem, making her the third ghost to become attached to me in some way I had no idea how to reverse. Worse, no one else could see her, so she spent far too much of her time pestering me to keep her amused.

Amber felt cheated, and since I was the only person who seemed to have any effect on her current state, she'd devoted her life after death to getting me to provide her with new experiences. Mostly she wanted me to take her on a trip to Paris, or, failing that, to entertain her with mystery and intrigue.

My budget only covered one of those things.

Her methods of persuasion included annoying me at every turn and tossing the word *Paris* into at least one conversation a day. Clearly, she hadn't been much of a people person, and death hadn't changed her into one.

"You know, I've read about people who came back from the dead, and for the most part, they were nicer to others after their experience. What's your deal?" The morning crankiness got my blood flowing.

"Duh, I didn't come back from the dead," she said, rolling her eyes. "Wait, are you saying I'm not a nice person?" Sometimes angry ghosts vibrate at a high enough frequency to make things happen in the physical world. Amber's annoyance shook a few icicles off the eaves.

"No," I sighed. "I'm saying you haven't been respectful."

"How is that different?"

Molly, my chocolate Lab, barked sharply at Amber, and Blue, who was staying with me while my parents took a short trip to Vermont, whined. Dogs, according to online sources, can see ghosts. Mine can, but I wasn't sure if Blue was reacting to Amber or to Molly. Older, and placid as a calm pond, Blue preferred to let the humans do what they did so long as there were treats and feet to cuddle. Molly was a little more demanding.

"I don't know, but it's not the same." I pulled up my collar against the chill.

"That doesn't even make sense." Amber's good mood returned, and the tiny hairs on the back of my neck settled back into place. "You're funny in the morning."

I glared at her because *funny* was not how I would have described how I was feeling. Static sparked between my layers as I shed my coat, sending little shocks down my back. I shivered.

"I live for your amusement," I grumbled and

followed the dogs back inside. "What are the chances," I said to Molly, "of you dogs letting me go back to bed for an hour or two? Emergency at the house on Tulip kept me up half the night." That last was for Amber's benefit.

"What kind of emergency?" she asked.

"Kids must have pulled some of the insulation out of the crawlspace, and the water pipes froze. I was up half the night trying to find a plumber, and then I had to fix it myself. Hence the current cranky mood."

What I didn't say out loud was that I wished David Barrington, who owned the Tulip Street house, and my parents weren't all in Vermont for the New Year. Not only would David have thawed the pipes, but he would also have handled the insulation at the same time. And I wouldn't have had to shimmy around in a narrow space with a blow dryer on an extension cord. Or drive home in the wee hours of the morning, put my surely spider-infested clothes in the washer, and take a shower to rid myself of a lingering case of the heebie jeebies.

"Sorry. I was with my dad. I didn't know." Amber confirmed something I hadn't wanted to ask. Namely, where she spent her nights. At least she wasn't breaking one of my cardinal rules and lurking around my place, watching me while I slept.

"Now, you do." By now, Molly was doing the dance of the perpetually empty stomach, and Blue was staring at me with naked longing, so I filled their empty bowls. "Look, Amber, I did my part in solving your crime, so why don't you do yours? Go into the light. I'm sure it's nice there."

"Not until I return the favor and help you solve yours. Then I'll go."

Amber referred to a somewhat knotty legal situation my ex-husband had done his level best to pin on me, and while I appreciated her help, I had a crack lawyer on my side already. What did I need with the ghost of a former reporter?

Nothing, really, but trying to tell her that was about like talking to a post.

"I appreciate the offer, but you really don't have to stick around on my account. I'll be just fine on my own." I spoke the truth, but Amber wasn't buying it.

"Really? Then you're aware that the white van that's been sitting in the church parking lot the past two days is the FBI? They're staking you out."

"I'm sure they're just watching to see if Paul makes contact," I bluffed and schooled my features so she wouldn't know I'd been blindsided by the information. "In any case, I've nothing to hide."

Amber shot an eyebrow up. "Everyone has something to hide. People do the stupid, they don't want anyone to know about. It's human nature."

"Fine." Giving up on any chance of another hour's worth of bedtime, I decided to make breakfast. Food would fill the hollow space in my gut that came from lack of sleep. Maybe.

"Of course, there are things I'd rather keep private, but there's nothing that pertains to the case against Paul. The feds know everything, and Agent Sully said he believed me when I explained how things worked. Raising the money was my job, someone else was in charge of spending it. Proving I'd been a victim of forgery didn't hurt my case, either. I don't think they're looking at me for fraud. I really don't."

Since I didn't trust my attention span to last long enough for cooking eggs at the moment, I dumped cereal into a bowl while Amber appraised me.

"Doesn't matter," she replied, hovering near the sink, "as long as they think you know something, you're on the hook."

"Well, I don't."

"Or maybe you don't know what you know. Or only think you don't know what you aren't sure you know."

I squinted at her and tried to follow the logic, but my sleep-deprived brain rejected the attempt. "You're not making sense, and I'm too tired for torture by talking."

Apparently, Amber took offense. "I was only trying to help."

"If you wanted to help, you'd have let me sleep until more than half of my brain cells were restored."

Amber bristled and made the air tingle with her ire. "I said I was sorry, what more do you want? I never left a story in the middle, and I don't intend to now, either. I need to see how this all plays out."

"This isn't a story," I said to her fading form. "It's my life."

Left alone, and halfway through my second cup of coffee, the caffeine finally tickled out a burst of coherent thought.

Why was the FBI watching my house? Considering the possibilities, I came up with very few variations on the one I'd mentioned to Amber earlier and one that didn't bear thinking about. Maybe they weren't watching me so much as watching over me.

Wasn't that a cheery thought?

But once lodged in my head, it was a notion that refused to be dispelled.

I tried. You have to give me credit for the effort. I pondered while I showered and dried my hair. I ruminated while I got dressed. I mulled over my options while pulling out the ornament boxes in preparation for taking down the Christmas tree, and decided to leave it alone. Let them sit out there and do whatever they wanted.

That lasted about half an hour.

"Forgive me, Patrea." I grabbed the last container of leftover Christmas cookies from the counter, hoped they weren't stale, and put on my coat. My attorney, Patrea Heard, would kill me if she knew I planned to offer treats to the feds without her there to make sure I didn't say anything to incriminate myself. Which I wouldn't since I hadn't done anything wrong.

My ex-husband Paul, however, must have used his family's charitable foundation as his own personal financial playground. When one of the donors began to suspect funds had been funneled back into the family coffers, he raised a stink, and because I had been the director of fund-raising, Paul had tried to hang me out to dry.

If not for Patrea's history with the family and her sharp eye for forgeries, I'd have probably spent Christmas in the slammer. Or maybe not, since Paul hadn't, as far as I knew, been arrested yet. Maybe there wasn't enough of a case against him, or perhaps I was closer to swinging in the wind than I thought.

Either way, I meant to find out.

CHAPTER TWO

mber had nailed the weather report. It wasn't even noon yet, but the air already burned my cheeks and practically made my eyelids creak. Even the sun looked chilled as it rode low in the eastern sky.

It occurred to me that whoever was stuck in that white van had a thankless job if they were required to spend a day as cold as this hunkered down in tight quarters. Still, these were the people invading my privacy, so I didn't work too hard at mustering up a ton of sympathy.

Instead, I let my boots crunch over snow and ice. They'd been watching my house, so they knew I was coming. No need for stealth.

The front of the cargo van slanted low enough to give me a view of the empty cab that reminded me of the one I'd rented to move back to Mooselick River. Well, except behind the seats of this one, access to the rear was blocked off by a small door. I cupped my hands and took a closer look in the front windows. The cab was empty, and I mean empty. There wasn't even a loose thread on the upholstery. The van looked abandoned.

Right. Like someone would abandon a vehicle like this in a small-town church parking lot.

My mittens muffled the sound when I banged on the sliding door.

"Agent Sully. Agent Coville. Open up. I know you're in there."

Being ignored really ticks me off. I went around to the back and tried banging on those doors but was met with the same response. Dead silence.

Mooselick River is a small town. You could probably tell that just from the name alone, but even in small towns, someone pounding on a vehicle and shouting at possibly imaginary occupants will eventually draw attention. After the curtains twitched back in the second of the nearest houses, I took the hint and stomped back home, fuming all the way.

Amber was wrong. That was it.

The problem was, my intuition said she wasn't.

Still, the fire of annoyance burned off the last traces of late-night fatigue and carried me through hauling out the Christmas tree—with a little help from Molly. Or rather, with some hindrance. The dog hadn't cared about the tree while it was standing, hadn't bothered a single ornament, but the sight of it tipped on its side in the snow was something else entirely.

Apparently, in that position, the tree represented a threat. One that must be subdued with all due haste and alacrity. She pounced, she growled, she grabbed the branches with her teeth and tried to shake the thing to death. Blue took one look at Molly, turned soulful eyes on me, and settled in the sunniest spot on the porch to watch. If she'd been a human, she might have rolled her eyes.

"Get it, you silly dog." I pulled out my phone to capture Molly's antics on video and noted I'd missed a text notification from my best friend, Jacy.

—*Do you have your dad's chili recipe?*

—*You'll get heartburn.* I warned.

She must have been practically sitting on her phone. *I don't care. The baby wants spicy food. Hot enough to make my teeth sweat.*

Jacy's my best friend. I'd kill to protect her, die for her if I had to, but the chances were good she'd take one look at the chili and decide the baby didn't want it after all. It would be faster to raid my parent's freezer than to make a batch from scratch, and since my dad never made less than a double recipe, I was sure that at least one container occupied the icy depths.

Consider it done.

Jacy sent back a swath of heart emojis while I added another item to my to-do list.

"Okay, Molly girl, I think you've killed that tree dead enough." I had to tug on her leash to get her to go inside, the lure of the tree was that strong.

Thankfully, Chris Evergreen had offered to pick it up and drop it at the goat farm out on Edes Road for me. One of the perks of introducing my lawyer to the owner of the Christmas tree farm when she'd ended up staying with me for the holidays. Watching the two most prickly people on the planet meet, circle each other like wary hedgehogs, and fall in love almost restored my faith in relationships.

For other people, of course.

Finding my husband in bed with one of my closest friends had shaken the foundation of my thoughts on love. Then, to heap more pain on top of misery, he'd forged my initials on an addendum to our prenuptial agreement. And all of that was before he'd tried to frame me for misappropriation of chari-table funds. A real peach, that one.

The guy was a jerk. Plain and simple. I knew that in the logical part of my brain, but I couldn't escape the fact that I hadn't seen through him before he blew my life to pieces. He'd sent me running home with barely more than the clothes on my back, and even though I'd landed on my feet, I wasn't ready to trust myself to anyone again.

Not yet, anyway. And not while the F—freaking—BI was staking out my house. Wouldn't that be quite the ice breaker on a first date?

Yeah, I can just see how it would go.

Hi, I'm Everly. I'm under investigation for money laundering, but I swear I didn't do it. Oh, and if that isn't enough, I bought a haunted house for the back taxes, only the house wasn't haunted, so that was a big win.

It is, though, but the amended version of my introduction wasn't any better.

Hi, I'm Everly. I help ghosts find peace, whether I want to or not. There might be one near me right now. Don't you want to take me out on a date?

Oh yeah, I'm a catch. Any man who heard just half of my story and didn't leave skid marks on his way out the door would be the kind of man I'd look sideways at because he'd clearly have lousy judgment.

So no, despite the fact my divorce had been final for several months, and my mother had been making subtle noises about fixing me up, I had no intention of dipping my toes in the dating pool.

These were my thoughts as I fired up old Sally Forth.

Yes, I named my car. Lots of people do; they just don't always admit to it. Sally had come to me along with the aforementioned house I'd bought right after moving back to town. It was an impulse purchase, you know, the kind near the register.

Laugh if you must, but it all happened just that quickly. I went to the town office to check the bulletin board for apartments to rent and unwittingly fell prey to the machinations of one Martha Tipton. I still think, though she refuses to confirm my suspicions, that she knowingly bamboozled me with her story about some unscrupulous person who wanted to buy Catherine Willowby's house only to tear it down.

Tear down Spooky Manor? Not on my watch.

I don't call it that anymore, in case you're wondering. Even though ghosts follow me home from time to time, there's nothing spooky about the house itself unless you consider a closet full of mannequin heads spooky, and then I guess there is. There was a reason for them, but that's a whole other story.

Anyhow, when I bought the place, old Sally was in the garage, and therefore considered part of the contents that came with my home-buying experience. My father hated that I drove a classic car in winter, but Sally got me from place to place, and I didn't have to make car payments.

I pulled into the grocery store parking lot and scored a space right near the door—which was odd enough for a Saturday, and downright strange on a holiday where liquor and food tend to be part of the festivities. Inside, the place looked like a ghost town. The Christmas version. Piles of red and green packaged treats filled a couple of shopping carts carrying signs offering a 50 percent discount.

Barking coughs punctuated the leftover Christmas music playing over tinny-sounding speakers, the liquid sound of phlegm sending me in search of disinfecting cart wipes. I considered slapping one over my face for extra protection, then decided I didn't want to be *that* person.

Five minutes, in and out, shallow breaths. I could do this.

I grabbed a couple of extra wipes and moved deeper into the germ zone. When the store's butcher came out with a tray of packaged chicken, a surgical mask covering his mouth, his eyes fever-bright, I hastily amended my party menu. Prepackaged meatballs versus scratch-made from plague-burger? That was a no-brainer. Plus, the time saved could translate to a short nap.

And with that thought in my head, I opted for bags of precut veggies for dipping. A minute saved was a minute snoozed.

"Hey, Robin." Since my former co-worker stood behind the only open register, I couldn't avoid a moment of inane chit-chat.

"Hey, you." Or maybe I could. She looked at me as if I'd just rolled in from out of town. We'd worked together for several weeks until our boss was murdered, so you'd think she'd at least remember my name. Then again, with all that air rushing around in her head, maybe not.

Robin scanned my items, pushing them along without paying attention to how they piled up at the end of the checkout area.

"It's quiet in here today," I observed as I ran my debit card through the reader.

Since she made no move in that direction, I began to bag my own groceries.

"Flu." Gum, the same color as the polish on Robin's nails, snapped and popped between her teeth. I could tell because she chewed with her mouth open. "We're short-staffed, but I guess it doesn't matter since no one's out and about anyway."

The lack of traffic as I drove away bore out Robin's observation. Mooselick River had gone quiet. Not that it was a metropolis of any sort to begin with, but driving through town and being almost the only one on the road seemed eerie.

Not as eerie as turning down my parent's street and nearly running over a too-small body in the road.

My heart stopped and then lurched into high-speed mode.

"Not again," I said out loud, panic and foreboding sending adrenaline coursing through my veins as I yanked Sally off to the side and applied the brakes. I barely got her into park before I was out the door and running to the prone form of the child lying face-down in the street. Maybe this time, I wouldn't be too late.

Somewhere, in a remote part of my brain, there was a voice warning me I didn't want to see what I was about to see. I hushed it and, not daring to turn the child over in case I caused more harm, reached to check for signs of life.

Had my head not been pounding with the sound of my own heart, I would have known right away that I wouldn't find a pulse. I would have recognized the flannel shirt and pants.

But no, I didn't trip to the deception until my fingers met a wooden post where the neck should have been.

Disgusted, I flipped the doll over.

The smaller towns in Maine aren't always on what you'd call the cutting edge of trends. And since the Shy Kids Dolls spoke to both the lawn art crowd and the crafty types, they were still a part of the land-scape, as it were.

A bit of stuffing over a rough form, some clothes, a backward baseball cap, and you've got yourself a cute little fella hiding his face against a tree or a fence...or the ice-covered pavement in this case. It had probably blown off someone's front porch just in time to freak me out.

Nothing like a little panic in the afternoon to get the blood flowing.

A combination of chagrin and annoyance followed me through my parent's house to the chest freezer, where I unearthed two containers of chili, and back to the kitchen where I left my dad a note to say I'd filched some of his stash.

Back home, I shook off the ominous feeling, prepped my food for the final game night of the year, and even managed a catnap. I woke up an hour later with only one thing left of my to-do list, and for once, I'd saved the worst for last.

Sighing, I retrieved Patrea's Christmas gift and laid the box on the kitchen table. What did I need with a video security system anyway? I had Molly, and she'd already proved herself ready to defend her territory.

Still, not even a chocolate Lab could go up against a pit bull like Patrea, and that meant I'd better hook up the system. The box had the words *Easy Installation* splashed across the front in a big, orange banner. Underneath, in smaller print, it said: Basic hand tools required. I sighed again and opened the box.

Not one to skimp, Patrea had gone for the deluxe model with four wireless cameras and a big controller unit. The thing had night vision, for Pete's sake, and motion detectors, and I could run it from an app on my phone.

In other words, total overkill.

Whether I needed it or not, she'd expect to see her gift in use when she showed up for the party, so I grumbled about it, but hauled out the stepladder and mounted one of the cameras near the front door. I even admitted, if only to myself, the box hadn't lied. Four screws in the base and a bit of adjusting was all it took. I mounted the second camera on the back porch facing the lawn, the third under the eaves of the garage to cover the driveway.

And then there was one.

"How much danger can I be in when the FBI is watching my house?" I asked Molly. As usual, she tilted her head but declined to answer.

Knowing they were out there should have put my mind at ease, but all it did was set my blood pressure soaring. And then I had an idea. "I wonder how they'd feel if the tables were turned." Again, Molly kept her opinion to herself, but she followed me up to the tower room.

"The box says these things have a range of a hundred feet."

Molly rubbed her head on my leg as I looked out the window. Now, I'm not really all that good with distances, but I figured the hundred feet might just about cover the FBI van, and if not, well, it was worth a shot.

I made a great show of setting up the camera, angling it just so. If they really were watching, I wanted Coville and Sully to know I wasn't fooled. Triumphantly, I flicked the power switch on and pumped my fist when the light turned green.

"Let's see how you like being watched." I checked the phone app. During the day, at least, the van was perfectly visible. In another couple of hours, we'd see if the night vision held up.

CHAPTER THREE

The rest of Jacy followed her belly into the house. The white, fleecy coat belted over the baby bump gave her the appearance of a snowman come to life.

"Don't try to hug me," she warned. "Peanut is in a kicky mood today. Nailed me in the ribs so hard I could hear it. Besides, you won't be able to reach, and somehow, I find it depressing when it takes two or more people linking hands to form a circle around me."

"Oh, come on. You look radiant." I hugged her anyway, and my arms fit around her well enough.

Sweeping back a fall of honey blonde hair, Jacy raised an eyebrow, but her eyes twinkled. "Everyone keeps saying I'm glowing. I'm not. That's sweat. It takes a lot of effort to haul myself anywhere given I'm approximately the size of a Clydesdale."

"Well, I can see you haven't lost your sense of humor." I looked at what she wore.

Blue text splashed across the front of Jacy's pink maternity top asked, *does this baby make me look fat?*

"No, but she has misplaced it once or twice." Brian grinned to soften what might have sounded like criticism. "Mostly on my account."

I envied the fond look that passed between them—a look that spoke of shared jokes and a solid bond. Paul and I had never been that comfortable with each other. How had I not seen that from the start? Or how thin the layer of his charm had been. It didn't matter now; I would never be that gullible again.

The doorbell shook me out of the early stages of a good brood, and if my smile was a little forced when I opened the door to let Neena in, I didn't think she noticed.

"Hey." Neena pulled off a knitted hat in the same deep blue as her eyes. A mass of dark and curly hair fell to her shoulders. We'd become close over the past few months. Well, as close as you can be to a woman who never suffered from hat hair.

"I brought wings and mushroom puffs." The music of the south wove through her voice as she handed me an insulated carrier to hold while she stripped off her coat. "Does it have to be this cold?"

Comfortable in my house, Neena grabbed the container back and headed for my kitchen.

"You're making me look bad," Jacy called after her. "I didn't cook."

Brian opened his mouth, but Jacy cut him off. "Don't say it." She wagged a finger at him, but a smile played around the corner of her lips.

"I have to." He took a step back to put himself out of reach. "Sure, you did. You've got a bun in the oven."

Upon uttering the one pregnancy phrase he knew his wife could not abide, he went back out to the car to retrieve two bottles of sparkling cider while Jacy glared mock daggers at his back.

The mood was high as I followed Jacy into the kitchen to watch Neena pull the foil off a pan of chicken wings that smelled so good it was criminal.

"What's in here?" Neena pointed to the first of several family-sized crock pots—thank you, Catherine, for being a hoarder—sitting on my countertop.

"Barbecued meatballs. The theme of the night is appetizers and finger food."

Jacy reached around her to pop the cover off the pot with the chili. "This is what I've been waiting for." She grabbed a bowl and a ladle. "We're okay to eat now, right? Peanut wants the hot stuff."

I laughed and waved her on. "Just remember to pace yourself."

She dug in with gusto while Neena lifted lids to inspect the rest of the offerings.

"The last one is sort of a cheese fondue thing. "

"Nothing like starting the year off with clogged arteries." Brian must have let Patrea and Chris in when he'd come back from the car. By now, the two men were probably in the living room talking sports.

I hugged Patrea hello and said, "There's a veggie platter in the fridge, Your Pickiness, and I used low-fat sour cream to make the dip." I didn't toss out a *so there* at the end, but it was implied.

Stepping back, I studied Patrea while Neena and Jacy talked in low voices about how much business they'd done for the day. Their shop, part secondhand store, part art gallery, had been as dead as every-where else in town.

"What? Is my shirt on inside out or something?"

"No," I replied, giving her the once-over. She wore jeans, a relatively new look for her, and a soft sweater in a shade that set off her eyes. Eyes no longer framed by lines of tension. "You look happy. It's good? With Chris, I mean."

"Very good." She nodded.

I couldn't help it; I pried. "Like *break into song in the grocery store* good?"

"Better."

I'd planned to tell her about the FBI van but decided that could wait. I didn't have the heart to wreck her mood. Time enough for that when she didn't look contented as a cat with a bowl of cream.

"What have we got for eats?" Brian's first glance upon entering the room went to Jacy. It happened every time, and I doubted he even realized he did it—that quick check to make sure she was there and the little smile that came when she was. "Something smells good."

We ate, we talked, we decided what games to play, and even though I was sure she'd moved on to the next plane of existence, I thought Catherine would approve of the way the house rang with laughter.

Later, while the men were setting up the whiteboard for Win, Lose, or Draw in the living room, Neena cornered me over the pot of fondue. "Did you hear the latest gossip?" Expertly, she whirled a pretzel rod through the smooth, cheesy sauce, then wrapped a pepperoni slice around the cheese and took a bite.

"I heard Viola's getting up a petition to have the school board erect a statue of Hudson out by the football field."

Neena shook her head. "That's old news. She went after Harley Thomas at the VFW Christmas party, and he told her it wasn't gonna happen even if she got the Pope to put his name down. The best they could do, he said, was put Hudson's name on a brass plate and dedicate one of the sections of bleachers to him."

"Are things still good between you and her?"

Viola Montayne was Neena's mother-in-law. When Neena's husband Hudson had been killed the previous June, Viola had done everything in her power to drive her son's widow out of town. The two grieving women finally managed to come together over Christmas, but with Viola, Neena would probably always be on precarious footing.

"Oh, as long as I let her think she's got some say over me, we'll get along. We both loved her son, after all. That gives us common ground."

I wished I hadn't brought up Viola and reminded

Neena of her loss. Though I supposed thoughts of Hudson were never far from her mind. He'd been my first ghost, but I didn't intend to tell Neena that particular story.

As far as she and everyone except for Jacy was concerned, a freak event saved me from being strangled by Hudson's killer. Who would believe me if I said his ghost had thrown a mannequin head down the stairs and knocked out the man who'd had his hands around my throat?

"Anyway," Neena continued, "you know the storefront next to the tackle shop has been empty since Natalie closed the yoga studio three years ago, right? Well, there's been activity in the building this week."

In the middle of our speculating whether Natalie might reopen the studio, Jacy let out a moan.

"What?" One look at her, and I called for Brian. "Something's wrong with Jacy."

"It's nothing." She made an effort to turn the grimace on her face into a reassuring smile. "Just those Braxton Hicks contractions. They come and go. I talked to my doctor, and she says it's nothing to worry about." Except she barely got the words out before another one hit hard enough to steal her breath. "These are just stronger than normal." The next forced another moan from her, and Brian wasn't having it.

"Then we'll just go on over to the Emergency room and make sure. Everly, can you get her coat?"

When I returned with hers, I had mine as well. "I'm coming with you."

"Me, too." Neena and Patrea spoke at once.

"Why don't I hang out with the dogs? I'll keep an eye on things here if that's okay with Everly." Chris offered.

"Thanks," I mouthed to him as we all headed for the door.

CHAPTER FOUR

Mooselick River doesn't run big enough to have a hospital, but the next town over does, and I'm pretty sure Brian broke two laws and a land speed record getting us there in under fifteen minutes. We pulled right up to the sliding doors, but before we could get Jacy out of the car, a man wearing green scrubs and a surgical mask came out to meet us.

"What's your emergency?" He sounded harried.

"My wife is having Braxton Hicks, but they're stronger than normal, so we wanted to make sure everything is okay." Brian reached in to help Jacy out of her seat.

"Wait," the nurse, or maybe it was a doctor—I couldn't really tell—practically elbowed Brian out of the way and talked directly to Jacy. He asked her a few questions about where she hurt, used hand sanitizer he pulled from his pocket, and checked her temperature and pulse.

"Listen, I could get into trouble for this, but I'm telling you for your own good, take her to Pine State Medical Center. The flu didn't hit as badly there, and they have a larger staff, so they won't be nearly as busy as we are."

"That's half an hour away. She needs to see someone now," Brian said.

"We're understaffed and overrun with this flu epidemic. The waiting room is full of patients, triage is stacked up, and we're minutes from having to close the ER to non-trauma patients. She'll be seen faster at PSMC even with the drive. Especially since I'll call ahead and see what I can do to fast-track the process."

When Brian would have argued, Jacy pulled her feet back inside and told him to get back in the car. "There are actual sick people in there. Stop wasting this man's time and let him get back to work. You're being ridiculous. I don't need to go to the hospital."

"Well, you're gonna." When Brian makes a decision, he's a hard man to sway.

"Do you want me to call Momma Wade?" Since I'd run tame in her house from the age of five on, Jacy's mother insisted I use the same title her kids used.

"No." Jacy barely took the time to consider. "I'm sure it's nothing serious, and having her show up to burn sage over me won't solve anything. If something's actually wrong, and I know it isn't, then you can call her."

While she had a deft hand with brewing up effective herbal remedies, Leandra did tend to go overboard with the smudge stick at times.

By the time we were halfway there, Jacy was no longer in a frame of mind to argue about anything. The pain had gone from intermittent to constant, and every wince or moan made Brian put on a little more speed. He shaved some time off the trip, and once the car rocked to a stop, even the unflappable Patrea had to pry her fingers off the spot she'd been clutching.

"We probably should have come in separate vehicles," Neena said, lines of worry etched into her forehead.

Brian helped Jacy out of the car, and when, after a few steps, she bent over double in pain, simply scooped her into his arms and strode through the sliding doors calling for someone to come and help. Following closely behind him, I thought I recognized one of the faces we passed, but it was only a fleeting thought at the time.

Between Jacy's moaning and Brian's loud insistence that his wife needed help *now*, and that someone should have called ahead about her, we got enough attention to skip triage and be sent straight back to a cubicle.

Just as Brian leaned to settle his wife down on the gurney-style bed, she made a strangled sound, stiffened, and, as my Grammie Dupree used to put it most delicately, Jacy broke wind.

It was long and loud, and in Jacy's case, highly embarrassing because that was the moment the doctor walked through the door.

"Oh," Jacy sounded surprised when the gas had all passed. "I feel better."

Silence held for a beat.

The doctor's lips twitched at the corners, just a little before she controlled her face and said, "I should hope so. Since you're here, let's just check a couple of things, though."

"We'll be in the waiting room." Neena, Patrea, and I beat a hasty retreat, and to our credit, I think 90 percent of the fit of laughter came from stress relief and wasn't at Jacy's expense. Okay, half, but that's my final offer.

A poker-faced nurse buzzed us out of the treatment area and into the waiting room shared by the ER and the imaging department, and her dour expression did nothing to contain the hilarity. What did put a lid on it for me, though, was seeing grief and fear on that familiar face in the waiting room.

"You're Alicia, right? Albert Runyon's daughter." Her name finally popped into my head.

Alicia nodded. "You're Everly Hastings."

"Dupree," I corrected automatically, but I don't think she heard me as she sobbed and launched herself into my arms. Knocked the giggles right out of my companions, too.

Dread settled into the pit of my stomach. "Alicia, honey, what happened?" I couldn't remember if there was a Mrs. Runyon still in the picture, but it didn't seem like Alicia had anyone else with her.

"It's my dad. I know it's bad, and they won't tell me anything."

I gave her a squeeze, then pulled back to look into eyes dark with fear in a face gone chalk white. "What happened?"

"He's been in a coma since just after school let out. A mugging gone bad. That's what the police officer said who came to my door. Someone beat my daddy with a bat or a tire iron, emptied his wallet, and left him to die in the street. Who does that?"

The security guard at the office where I had also worked for my ex-husband's family, Albert had treated me with kindness on the worst day of my life. I felt bad now that he'd spend the last few months fighting for his.

"I'm so sorry. I didn't know. Is there anyone I can call for you?"

Alicia shook her head. "No, but thank you. My aunt Denise has been staying with me, but she had to go back to St. Louis to take care of some stuff. She's only been gone a couple of days."

"I'm so sorry."

"I called as soon as they brought him down here for scans, and she's trying to get a flight out. She'll be here as soon as she can." She looked toward the doors we'd just come through. "I've been waiting for three hours. He's still in there, and they won't tell me anything."

Over the girl's shoulder, I saw Patrea put on her lawyer face—jaw set, eyes no-nonsense flat. "Excuse me," she said to the nurse. "We need some information on a patient."

She looked to me, and I supplied the name. "Albert Runyon."

"I'm sorry, ma'am. I'm not allowed to give patient information to non-family members."

"That's his daughter," Patrea said, her tone ringing with scathing authority. "I assume she's considered a family member."

Nurse Cranky changed her tack. "She's a minor, and I'm not sure if I should—"

"Well, then, let's get some clarification on that." Patrea pulled out her phone and began scrolling through her contacts list. "From the Chief of Medicine." Her finger hovered over the call button. I felt a little sorry for exposing the nurse to Patrea in scary-lawyer mode, but not that much. She'd put Alicia through hours of agony, so my sympathies were in short supply.

"Let me just get someone for you." She paged someone from imaging who gave us at least a tidbit of information, and whatever she said to whoever called her right back had Dr. Maron swinging down the hallway only minutes later.

"Miss Runyon. We can talk in here." He indicated a small room marked private on the door and stepped back to let her proceed ahead of him.

"Is it okay if ... Everly, would you come in with me?"

"You'll let Jacy know if she comes out?" I glanced back at Neena, who nodded, then followed Alicia into the room.

"If he's gone, could you just please say it fast and get it over with? I can't take any more waiting." If Alicia went any paler, she'd turn translucent.

"Your father is showing significant changes in brain activity. These are positive signs, and he has gained several points on the Glasgow coma scale," he said, and I heard the *but* coming. Alicia probably did, too. "But he's still only showing localized cognitive response."

Alicia started to ask the question most on her mind, but he held up a hand to stop her. "I can't tell you if or when he will regain full consciousness because I don't like putting limits on patients. My job is to give him the best care I can, his is to have the will to heal."

"This is good, though, right?" Alicia said, hope coloring her features. "It sounds like he's getting better."

"With traumatic brain injury, we can repair a lot of the immediate damage. Then it's up to the patient.

I don't want to hold out false hope because I've seen patients show signs of recovery, and then relapse or die. I don't think that will be the case this time, but you should be prepared for every eventuality. If and when he wakes up, he'll have a period of rehab ahead of him. We just won't know until we know."

Taking pity, though, Dr. Maron offered, "This is only an educated guess, but I'd say two or three days at most, and we'll have more answers."

I reached for Alicia's hand, gave it a squeeze to stop the trembling. She said, "Thank you."

We both watched Dr. Maron's face as he opened the chart he carried and made a notation.

"We've done a CT, and based on what I saw, I've ordered an MRI. I'll talk to you again as soon as I've had a chance to look at the results. Meanwhile, he's being transported back upstairs. Are you ready to go up? Or did you have more questions?"

"No. I need to see him. I can stay in the room, right? For the next few days like I did when he first arrived."

"Yes, of course." Dr. Maron's gaze landed on me. "Too many visitors at once might be too much stimulation."

I hugged Alicia, and we exchanged numbers. "I

know people say this all the time, but I really do mean it. Call me if you need anything, and keep me posted on your father's condition. I'll be praying for him."

"Is that the same Albert who worked for Paul?" Patrea practically pounced on me when I returned to the waiting area.

"It is. He's been in a coma since the summer. Traumatic brain injury. Someone attacked him with a baseball bat not too long after I left the foundation. I guess it was a little while before someone found him and got help." Picturing Albert lying hurt and alone broke my heart. "The doctor basically said it could go either way. He's showing increased brain activity, but that sometimes happens right before coma patients pass away."

"If it helps," Neena said, patting my hand, "if the doctor didn't mention transferring him to Eastern or Southern Maine, that means a lot. They'd have him in a 'copter right now if they thought they couldn't handle it here. That's a good thing."

The sliding doors opened to disgorge Jacy and Brian from the treatment area. She took one look at our solemn faces and said, "What's up?"

I filled her in while we waited for Brian to pull up

with the car, and because Jacy was ... well, Jacy, she decided we'd put together a care package for Alicia and bring it by the hospital the next day.

Considering the average wait in an emergency room situation, we'd managed to pull off a miracle and would be back at my place a couple of hours ahead of the new year. The ER doc hadn't done anything except ask a few questions. She'd warned against eating too many spicy foods and performed a New Year's miracle by releasing Jacy without even sending her to registration.

"Look," Jacy pointed out, "there's Taco Bell. Babe, can we hit the drive-up? Peanut is dying for a burrito."

"You're kidding, right?" Brian glanced over at his wife. "You just scared two years off my life and almost gave me a heart attack because Peanut wanted chili." His next question was directed at me. "What was in that stuff anyway? Industrial strength beans fortified to produce extra gas?"

Crammed in the back seat like sardines, I could feel Neena shaking with the effort to hold in her laughter because Brian had been truly upset by the whole ordeal.

"No, just regular beans." I realized a moment too late the question had been rhetorical.

"There will be," Brian said in a tone that suggested finality, "no more beans for peanut. Taco Bell is off the menu." Ignoring Jacy's longing look, he passed the entrance and pointed the car toward Mooselick River. And if Jacy hadn't chosen that moment to let out a final, very quiet, but still audible toot, Neena might have kept herself in check.

Even then, she gave it a heroic try, only to be undone by Patrea's snort. And then it was on.

"Turn around, I think I'm gonna die." Tears streamed down Neena's face as she clutched her middle. "And I didn't even try the chili."

When we got back to my place, amid half-hearted protests mostly from Jacy, Brian poured the pot of chili into the trash. Neena and Patrea regaled Chris with the story of Jacy's not-quite emergency while, under the watchful eye of her husband, the mother-to-be gorged herself on veggies. He allowed her one of the chicken wings—Chris had turned the oven down to just keep them warm and added a little water so they wouldn't dry out—and a single meatball. He slapped her hand away when she went back for another.

"See how that one settles first. Then you can have more."

She narrowed her eyes at him, then leaned over to plant a loud kiss on his lips. "You're going to be a good daddy. Ridiculously annoying and overprotective, but a good one."

He let her have the second meatball.

CHAPTER FIVE

We fit in a few rounds of Win, Lose or Draw, laughed a lot, and when the ball dropped at midnight, I silently marked its descent as a moment of acceptance that my life was changed—in most ways, for the better. I hadn't gone into my marriage looking for a man to control my life. But I'd let Paul take me over so slowly, so skillfully, that I hadn't noticed the reins slipping from my fingers. Taking them back hadn't been easy, but I'd done it, and with at least—depending on who you asked—a modicum of dignity.

Every ending carries with it the seed of a new beginning. Or, as my Grammie Dupree used to say when one door closes, another one opens, but if it doesn't, you just go throw a brick through the window.

Grammie was wise, but carried a certain disregard for the rules that I admired, envied, and in my youth, emulated. Not to the point of being wild, mind you. At least not by her standards.

Interrupting my moment of introspection, Neena pressed a glass of champagne into my hand and kissed me soundly on the mouth.

"There. I figure you're my date for the night, and since the New Year's kiss is a thing," she said, pointing a thumb over her shoulder at the two couples lip-locking, "I didn't want us to miss out."

"I know it's only been six months, but have you considered dating again?" Neena and I had become single at roughly the same time, though in different ways.

As soon as I saw the sadness wash over her face, I regretted asking, but she considered carefully before answering.

"In the abstract, yes, I have. But not seriously. Like, I'm not looking for anyone now, but I'm open to thinking about the possibility if it comes up later. Of course, I expect the whole town will call me a Jezebel given the situation we were in when Hudson died."

Temporarily separated at the time of his murder, Hudson had been staying at the Bide-A-Way Motel until he could prove to Neena that his gambling days were behind him.

"Don't let the gossip-mongers get in your head. You're the only one who can truly know when you're ready to date again. I think—no, I know—Hudson would want you to be happy." He'd told me as much before he went into the light. "Whenever that time comes."

"What about you? If the timing works out, we could be dating buddies. Or is that not a thing?"

Champagne bubbles tickled my nose as I slugged down half the glass. "Misery loves company, I suppose. And since I'm looking at the idea of dating as misery and not an adventure, I'd say I'm not ready."

"To living our best life," Neena toasted. "On our own terms."

I drank to that.

The party wound down fairly early by New Year's standards. Before she left, Patrea pulled me aside for a private word. "If anything changes with Albert before we do Jacy's care package run tomorrow, I want you to let me know, and I don't want you going back to the hospital alone."

"Okay, Mom."

Patrea narrowed her eyes mockingly. "I'm not

that much older than you." Still, she waited for me to agree to her request.

"I'll call if anything happens so you can come along."

"Make sure you do." She hugged me and followed Chris out the door.

I was just about to collapse into bed when my phone bonged out a text alert from Alicia.

—*No change. He's moving his arms more, and mumbling sometimes. I'm afraid to close my eyes.*

Alicia couldn't be much more than sixteen or seventeen since she'd taken the SATs a few days before the last time I'd talked to her father. She'd be partway through her senior year, and college-bound the next fall. Albert wanted an education for his daughter badly enough to work two jobs to keep her from being saddled with a ton of student loan debt.

Any word on your aunt's arrival? You shouldn't be alone, I sent back.

She's at the airport on standby for the next flight out, but it won't leave until six, and it lands in Portland. She'll rent a car and drive the rest of the way. We're looking at tomorrow afternoon earliest.

Just hang in there, honey, he's got you to fight for, and

he's a strong man. Try and get some sleep. You'll feel better for it.

I will. Thanks for being there. It helps. Dad was right. You are a nice person.

I sent up a little prayer for the family, thanked her, and said nice things about Albert until after a few minutes more, she thought she might be able to sleep a little. It took me a long time to do the same.

Six hours down was all I managed before the dogs wanted breakfast. The second thing I did after letting them out was to check in with Alicia. Still hanging out at the airport, her aunt had booked a flight for the next day but was still hoping a seat would open up before then. Albert's condition hadn't changed.

To make my morning more of a challenge, Amber popped in to give me the weather report while I drank my first cup of coffee. As she prattled on, I gathered there was no chance the storm hovering over the Midwest would blow itself out before sliding north and east. We were in for, as Amber termed it, a significant snow event that could be upgraded to a bomb cyclone storm if it dipped far enough south to hit the Atlantic before drifting north.

"Another cold one today, and you'll note the dogs were already up, so you can't blame your foul mood on me."

"I'm not in a foul mood." Distracted would be the better term since I'd been fielding texts from Jacy about what should go in the care package for Alicia.

Amber raised an eyebrow. "Maybe you should tell your face. It thinks you're in a bad mood. I was with my dad, thank you for asking."

And she was the one calling my mood dark?

"Something happened last night." I gave her the short version of events.

"That's the same Albert who quit or got fired after you did?" Amber zipped back and forth, her feet hovering inches above the floor. The ghostly version of pacing a room, I guessed. "Do you think there's a connection?"

"To what?" My brain still felt sludgy from two short nights of sleep in a row. "The office closed down, and Paul probably hired someone willing to take less money. I can't see how that had anything to do with me."

"No, you idiot, the accident, or mugging, or whatever. Maybe he knew something your ex-husband wouldn't want made public. Tell me everything about the last time you saw the man. Maybe there's a clue."

Amber stopped zipping back and forth and settled in one spot to listen.

"You're going to hurt yourself with these wild leaps of logic." My tone was dryer than a forgotten house plant, but Amber merely circled a hand to indicate I should start talking.

"There's not a lot to tell. I went to work, he stopped me before I could get on the elevator and told me he couldn't let me go up."

"But what did he say? What did you say to him? Give me a visual."

Pausing, I let the scene replay in my head. "I walked in and asked about his daughter. Alicia had taken her SATs, and I asked how she did. If he answered, I can't remember. Then he told me he couldn't let me go up to my office and very gently said I'd been fired. He was sorry, and I could tell he didn't like being the bearer of bad news."

Now that I'd dredged up pieces of the worst day of my life, more bits and pieces surfaced.

"He gave me a box of my things, and there was a weird moment."

"Now we're getting somewhere." Amber leaned forward. "What happened?"

Risking her ire, I paused again to bring the moment clear. "It wasn't what he said so much as the way he said it. 'I got them to let me collect your things.' His eyes went all intense or something. I was so blindsided, I just let him carry the box to my car, and I drove away. But it occurs to me now that it was odd."

"Well?"

I'd apparently paused again because Amber seemed impatient.

"Well what?"

"What was in the box? You really are worthless in the morning."

Amber earned herself a glare. "Nothing much. A house plant, the photos from my desk." I frowned trying to picture it. "My mother unpacked it, I think ... wait." I closed my eyes. "There was an envelope. One of those yellow ones."

"Okay," Amber drew the word out long. "What was in the envelope? I swear it's like trying to drag a mule over a mud puddle to get any information out of you."

Now I felt like the idiot she thought I was. "I didn't open it."

She let out a pained sigh. "Why on earth not?"

"Look," I snapped, my blood pressure kicked up a notch. "I had just been dumped, fired, found a dead body, become haunted, bought this house practically sight-unseen, and was moving in. All in the course of a week. Excuse me if one or two minor details fell through the cracks."

When I didn't jump right up, she said in a long-suffering tone, "Don't you think maybe you should take a look at it now?"

You can't burn a ghost with a look. I know, because I tried. Amber folded her arms and tapped her toes with a hollow, almost echo of sound.

"I would, but I don't know where it is." There, I admitted it. And I pinched the bridge of my nose to stave off the beginning of a tension headache. "The last time—the only time, really—I remember seeing it, it was on the counter with the plant and the name-plate from my desk."

Even though I knew the envelope hadn't been lying on my countertop for six months, my gaze still strayed in that direction.

"I have no idea what happened to it after that."

Still looking annoyed, Amber speculated. "It was probably your severance package. There might have even been a check in there."

That one made me snort and dispelled the tension around my eyes. "Can't sever what never existed. It was an unpaid position. Paul said taking the job was a good way to do my part for the family. The way he treated me during the divorce," I shook my head. "Let's put it this way, if there was a check in that envelope, I'd eat it on toast."

My phone rang before she could start in on me about finding the envelope, but I made a mental note to ask Jacy if she'd seen it while we were unpacking. Failing that, my mother might have put it away, and she'd remember where it was for sure. Kitty Dupree had a mind like a steel trap.

Sometime during the conversation with Jacy about whether I thought Alicia would prefer a pink or purple throw in her gift box, Amber faded out. I considered that a blessing, and when I pulled my attention back to the conversation, Jacy announced she would pick me up, and we'd go to the shop together to decide.

"Patrea sent a text earlier saying she has a container of baked goods, but asked if we would wait until late afternoon to go." While we talked, I headed upstairs and dug out a gift bag from the drawer where Catherine had kept them. Tucking the phone between my shoulder and ear, I went into the next room and began to fill the bag.

"Afternoon works for me. I don't have to collect rents until the bank opens on Monday, so I'm on call for emergencies, but otherwise, I'm free. I'm raiding the pack-rat cabinet in the upstairs bathroom for toiletries as we speak. Catherine certainly didn't skimp when it came to stocking up on toothbrushes and soaps. She had good taste in brands, too."

Jacy sighed. "I do wish I'd had a chance to know Mrs. Willowby better before she passed. If I'd known you would end up owning Spooky ... her house"— Jacy hastily amended the name we never used for my house anymore—"I'd have made more of an effort."

In a very real sense, Catherine Willowby had become my benefactor. I'd found some of her diaries, and having read a bit, knew how lonely she'd been toward the end of her life.

"She'd have loved you." Everyone did. Jacy was too sunny not to love.

Moving back to the original topic, Jacy said, "Neena's bringing magazines and a selection of books for Alicia to choose from. She has wide tastes, so something ought to suit. I think that should cover all the bases." I could all but hear the sympathy radiating across the phone. Jacy's heart was bigger than the sky.

CHAPTER SIX

The biggest thing about being haunted that I will never get used to is ghosts popping in whenever they feel like it. Amber had a habit of picking the worst times, too.

"I guess I missed moving day, so my services as a spy are no longer needed."

On my hands and knees with half my body inside the bathroom cabinet, I banged my head on the shelf above when Amber spoke.

"Ouch. Is it really necessary to sneak up behind me like that? You could see what I was doing, right? But still, you thought that cleaning cabinets was the perfect time for parsing cryptic comments from a pesky ghost." I rubbed my head where it had made contact with solid wood.

"Always with the drama. Your ex has moved," Amber said slowly as if I wouldn't understand the words without her drawing them out long. "I was just there two days ago, and there was no sign they were planning to leave. Everything in its place and nary a packed box to be seen."

"Nary a one, huh?" I couldn't help teasing her a little.

"There's nothing wrong with having a decent command of language, and that's not the point. There's a sold sticker on the sign out front, and they've already moved out. I missed it, and you know what that means."

I finally caught on. "It means you can't sneak around and check on Paul and Reva anymore because you haven't been where they are."

Amber grimaced. "I'm not sure you can call it sneaking when I walk right through the door, bold as brass. Just because they can't see me doesn't mean anything."

She meant through the door in the most literal sense. I didn't have the heart to point out she'd learned very little useful information up to now, or that I had no interest in hearing the way Reva cooed and stroked Paul's ego on a daily basis.

Or in talking about it anymore. "Nothing to do about it now."

"Sure, there is. You find out where they moved and take me there."

"Do you even hear what you're saying? The FBI is watching me, and you want me to stalk my ex-husband so you can do a little ghostly breaking and entering? No, okay? Just no."

I pointed to the jumble of items strewn over the bathroom floor. "If you'll excuse me, I have things to do today." Now that the cleaning bug had bitten me, I intended to finish with the bathroom and the medium bedroom.

In a huff, Amber faded out.

Midway through sorting the contents of yet another of Catherine's drawers, I heard Molly's less-than-delicate steps on the stairs. She barreled into the room, saw me, bunched her muscles, and flattened my stack of carefully folded handkerchiefs as she leaped and landed on the bed.

"Molly!" I began to chide her, but then saw her hackles were up, her fur ruffled all along her spine. "What's—" The doorbell rang. "Ah, someone's here. You could have just barked, you know. Then I wouldn't have more work to do."

I rose, and, happy that she'd done her job of alerting me, Molly sent the old bedsprings zinging with a second leap to the floor. Plastic eggs that had once contained pantyhose—and don't get me started on how odd a marketing idea that had been—flew like shrapnel. Two of them cracked open when they hit the floor to disgorge their contents, which were not pantyhose, but money.

That Catherine had been something of a hidden hoarder, I'd learned within a day of moving into the house. To the untrained eye, every room had looked relatively tidy, with only a few more doodads on the shelves and more furniture than strictly necessary. But every stuffed-to-the-brim drawer, cabinet, and closet told a different tale.

The doorbell rang again, followed by a hammering knock, and Molly growled.

"I'm coming!" I called as I headed down the stairs.

Patrea would have a fit, but I didn't use the security app to check who was standing on the porch. I merely opened the door and then slammed it shut again wishing I had.

"Where is he?" Reva, my nemesis. My former friend. The woman who'd broken up my marriage shouted through the door. "Paul! I know you're in there. At least be man enough to dump me in person."

I couldn't help it, I opened the door again. "Have you lost your mind? Paul isn't here."

"Are you sure?"

The spot between my eyes began to ache. "Of course, I'm sure. Don't you think I'd know if there was a lying, cheating weasel in my house? The smell alone would give him away."

It felt good to slam the door in her face a second time and would have felt better yet if that had been the end of it, but she rang the bell again.

"Open up, Everly. Please!"

"Go away, Reva. I have nothing to say to you."

Molly growled again. The dog had excellent taste in people.

"Please! I don't know where else to turn."

Was she crying? Miss I'm-Made-of-Stone never cried. I didn't trust it, or her.

But I opened the door out of morbid curiosity.

"What do you want? I told you Paul isn't here, so skedaddle." Positioning myself dead center of the opening, I left not even a spare inch for her to get past me. Not that she'd try with Molly standing guard.

Compared to the snotty way she'd acted the last time she'd landed on my doorstep, Reva looked like she hadn't had a good day. Some little part of me took pleasure in that. The rest of me didn't seem to mind.

"I know I don't deserve a second chance." She stared at my shoes as if unable to look me in the eye. "But I'm begging you for one anyway. We were friends once, and I need a friend right now. I need my best friend. I need you."

"Excuse me while I go find a shovel to clear that load of crap off my porch. What's your ulterior motive, Reva? Because I know you've got one." I folded my arms across my chest, tilted my head to the side, and glared at her.

She held up shaking hands. "I don't. I really don't. I'm just ... I'm sorry. For everything. I've wanted to say that for so long."

"Well, there, you've said it. You can go now and enjoy my ex with a clear conscience."

As far as I was concerned, she could have him, and that same little part of me hoped he did to her what he'd done to me. Or worse.

"No, I can't because Paul left me. He's gone, and I have nowhere to go, no money to pay for a place to stay, and no one else to turn to."

"So coming here with a lame apology is what, a bid for sympathy because you've been dumped by the man who dumped me? Did you think we were going to be solidarity sisters because we shared a crappy experience?" I barked out a short laugh. "You're out of luck because I have none for you. Not even a shred."

"I don't deserve it. I know that." Reva shivered dramatically. "Can't we go inside and talk? It's freezing out here."

I wanted to say no. I wanted to boot her off my porch, but I heard Grammie Dupree's voice as plain as day.

Keep your enemies close.

Good advice, I supposed. What with Paul trying to frame me for his crimes, Reva might know something that would help the feds finally pin him down for good. It wouldn't hurt my feelings a bit to be the one holding the key to his freedom. I could almost hear the cell door slamming behind him with a satisfying clang.

"I guess you can come in." Grudgingly, I stepped back to let her in. "But if you piss me off, I'll sic Molly on you, and this time, I won't pull her back."

Reva had no way of knowing that Molly was usually the gentlest of dogs. Their first and last experience together had been anything but gentle, but when you slap a dog's person, they often take great offense.

Chilled air and too much sickly-sweet perfume followed Reva inside where I didn't offer her a drink, or to take her coat, or any other pleasantry. She wasn't welcome, and I wanted her to know it.

"Okay, you wormed your way in here, so say what you came to say, and then leave," I ordered.

"You've changed," was the unexpected comment. "I never thought you'd turn into such a hard case." Reva's breath hitched, and her lip trembled. "I'm standing here begging for your forgiveness, and you couldn't care less. I never meant to hurt you."

My eyebrows went up in shock, then down in a frown. "So it was accidental sex you were having with my husband when I walked in on you?" Fingernails dug into my palms when my fists clenched hard.

"How did that go, exactly?" I didn't give her time to answer. "Wait, I know. Paul invited you up to admire the new sheets, and you both tripped on your way in, conveniently falling out of your clothing and landing on the bed together at an odd angle that I mistook for sex. Is that your story?"

"No." Reva pulled her collar up around her face. "I didn't say the relationship was an accident, just that I didn't plan to break up your marriage. It just sort of happened."

I shook my head to dislodge the fantasy of lightning striking her down where she stood and remembered another thing my Grammie Dupree used to say. *The best way to find out what's under the hood is to kick the tires.*

Okay, I know that makes no sense to anyone who has ever driven a car, but what she meant was the best way to see what a person is made of is to poke at them a little. Or maybe that wasn't really what she meant, and I just wanted to poke Reva to get some of my own back. Either way worked for me.

"Well, it's not difficult to tell what Paul saw in you. He gets off on knowing he's the smartest one in a relationship."

I left her an opening wide enough to drive a team of bulls through, but instead of taking it, her lip trembled again, and tears gathered. The kind I wanted to think were fake but seemed genuine enough.

"He's gone, and I don't know where he is. I almost hoped to find him here."

"Never!" I swore. "I would rather crawl across broken glass just to bathe in a tub of vinegar than spend five minutes with Paul."

There didn't seem much else to say on the subject, but Reva showed no signs of leaving. Not even when I said, "If you've said everything you came to say, I have things to do."

Drawers to sort, ghosts to help. You know, the usual.

"It's just … I thought … it's probably stupid to ask, but the house sold faster than we planned, so we were staying at a hotel until we found something else. But Paul took off, I guess, without paying. They asked me to leave, and now I don't have anywhere else to go. Since we're in sort of the same boat, I thought maybe you'd let me stay here."

"Here?" My eyes went so wide they hurt a little. "You want to stay here."

So many emotions, not the least of which was admiration for her having the guts to ask, and pity for her being just that stupid.

"No," I said without heat or inflection.

Keeping your enemies close is one thing, letting them sleep in your house is entirely another.

"The best I can do is get you a room at the Bide-A-Way for a night or two while you figure out your next move."

"Move," Reva repeated. She snapped her fingers

and her face cleared. "That's it. I know where Paul went. We were talking about moving to Denver. He probably flew out to look at a place and forgot his phone charger. That's why he's not answering calls. He'll come back for me in a day or two."

The Paul I knew wouldn't have moved to Denver, but then, the Paul I thought I knew wouldn't have hooked up with someone this foolish. And looking at real estate didn't explain the early checkout, but Reva smiled like she'd been given the world's largest lollipop.

"Two days at the most, and he'll come back for me. Let me stay here and try to make all this up to you. I want my friend back. I've missed you so much."

Even if I was tempted, which I wasn't, I couldn't have Reva in the house. I'd get whiplash trying to keep up with her changing moods.

"The Bide-A-Way. Three nights. Then you're on your own."

She started to protest, and I held up a hand to stop her. "I'll pay, and you'll find a way to pay me back later."

CHAPTER SEVEN

"Wait, we're buying pajamas for Alicia?" I didn't mention Reva's early morning visit or the fact that she was, even now, firmly ensconced in a room at the Bide-A-Way motel. Paying for her room might have been the stupidest thing I'd done in recent months, and I didn't need confirmation from outside sources.

"No, we're not. I am. I saw some in the to-be-sorted box. We haven't even tagged them in yet, but they're brand new. Still in the package, and I haven't seen any lot purchases on the books this week, so I'm thinking they should have been consignment items. I'll kick in the consignment percentage, and I'm sure Alicia won't mind since they've never been worn."

Following Jacy to the back room, I shivered as a sudden chill washed over my skin.

"Is there a draft in here? When David gets back from Vermont, we should have him check it out."

"I didn't feel anything." Jacy tossed me a puzzled look over her shoulder. "But I was going to ask him to look at that broken rack, so I can have him check for drafts at the same time. It always feels warm to me, but that could be a pregnancy thing."

Or it could be a ghost thing, I realized when I picked up one of the packages of pajamas and it felt as though it were coated in a thin layer of ice. "Who brought these in? Do you know?"

I risked a quick look around to see if I could catch a glimpse of a non-living eavesdropper. Amber knew the rules, and even though she ignored most of them, she did have the decency to keep her chilly self away from me most of the time. She might be annoyed by our earlier conversation, but this was not her.

"Not sure. They came in on my day off. You'd have to ask Neena." She held up two packages, one with a set of PJs in pink plaid flannel, the other a set in soft, gray fleece with pink trim. "Which one?"

"Go with the fleece. Hospital rooms tend to run chilly," I said offhandedly as I glanced around the room looking for other ghostly signs.

I'm not a medium or a psychic, but I am haunted. I've decided there's a distinction since I'd never seen so much as a flicker until Momma Wade meddled around with what she called my third eye. All my ghosts have been people I knew, too. So that was another point in haunting's favor.

Being haunted didn't mean I had some inherent ability, merely a run of bad luck and a spate of finding bodies. Well, except for Nick Mason's, but I did know him a little, and I'd been close by when fire and rescue pulled his body from the wreckage, so it came to the same thing.

Following that logic, my stomach lurched. Had someone died in the shop? Or outside?

"I have to—" Right in the middle of Jacy discussing the merits of two different throws, I walked away to prowl every aisle.

"What are you looking for?" Jacy waddled after me.

"Oh, nothing." I hoped. "Just getting the lay of the land."

"You fill in for me all the time. You're acting weird."

Maybe so, but I made sure the place was corpse-free anyway. You can't be too careful about these things.

"Let me see those pajamas again, please." Jacy knew about my recent ghostly history, and what's more, she believed me. Hard not to given her first-hand experience, but haunted pajamas might be a stretch even for her.

"Okay." Jacy handed me both of the sets she'd been trying to decide between just as Neena walked in through the back door.

"Hey, do you know, just off the top of your head, who brought these in? I'm assuming they were meant for consignment, or did someone come in with a lot to sell outright, and the purchase wasn't logged?"

Neena pulled off her gloves one finger at a time, then removed her knit cap before answering. Again with the lack of hat hair.

"Neither. Someone dropped off three bags of clothes and a couple boxes of other items on the back steps. That would have been last Tuesday."

Jacy sighed and offered a mild rebuke. "We don't take donations. Those should go to one of the churches."

"Oh, I think we'll make an exception in this case. I'm pretty sure I know where this stuff came from and why it was left here." Neena took one of the pairs of pajamas and laid it on the counter, then smoothed the plastic while she pulled herself together. "Justine Banner took the first offer that came in on her place, gave the real estate lawyer her power of attorney to do the deal, and left town last Tuesday."

As soon as I heard the name, I put two and two together and came up with the ghost.

The pajamas must have belonged to Felicity Banner, the victim of a hit-and-run accident her father had blamed on Nick Mason. Well, to be fair, the whole town thought he did it, but Dick had acted alone the day he forced Nick's truck off the road, sending the innocent young man to his death. And Nick had been innocent—or so he'd insisted while he haunted me.

The good of living in a small town outweighs the bad at least ninety percent of the time. The other ten percent, and I was sure Justine would agree, could rob a person of their sanity. Dickie Banner's arrest for manslaughter had been a hot topic since Halloween and would remain so until something juicier came along.

"Who could blame her for wanting to get out of Mooselick River? She's lost her daughter and her husband. A new start might be the best thing for her."

"So these pajamas," —I skimmed a finger over ice-cold plastic and repeated my earlier thought out loud— "must have belonged to Felicity." From there, it took almost no leap of logic to assume her mother dropped off more than just a few items she could no longer bear to look at.

Jacy's eyes were wide when she turned toward me, and I gave her a subtle shrug. I could be wrong. "Maybe we should pick something else for Alicia," she said.

"Why?" Neena frowned. "I only knew the family a little, but Felicity was a sweet girl. She'd want Alicia to have these and would be happy knowing they brought comfort to someone who needed it."

I felt the subtle shift of energy in the room and assumed that even though I'd yet to lay eyes on the ghost, she'd been listening. When the air warmed, I took the hint. "It's settled then." The pajamas went back into the bag just as a horn tooted outside the front door.

"That'll be Patrea. You two go on ahead and get Jacy settled. I'll lock up and be right out."

Once they'd gone, I took a moment to speak into

the emptiness. "I hope Neena's right, and you won't do anything to make Alicia feel uncomfortable. She's going through a lot right now. I'll come back as soon as I can and figure out a way to help you find the light, okay? Can you trust me to do that?"

I had no idea how I'd make good on the promise, but I hoped her silence meant yes.

Patrea insisted on driving. "No offense, Jace, but I'm not tooling through the city in the bubble-gum mobile. Not during daylight hours, anyway."

Not that the mini-van in Jacy's signature pink was the entire reason Patrea wanted to drive. She liked being in control, maybe even needed it. I wasn't complaining, though. An hour subjected to Jacy's brand of skill and reckless abandon behind the wheel would have pushed Patrea right over the edge.

It wasn't entirely Jacy's fault she was a heart attack on wheels. Brian's father, a man who had spent his twenties touring fairs around the country with a stunt show, had taught her to drive. If my parents had known Jacy could put a car up on two wheels and take a spin around the block, I'm pretty sure they'd have never let me leave the house with her again.

On the way, I regaled them with the abbreviated

version of Reva's visit. The only thing I left out was her current whereabouts.

When we arrived at the hospital, Jacy insisted on carrying one of the bags.

"Give that to me." Neena reached for the handle. "Don't you think you're carrying enough already."

"It was my idea." Jacy swatted at Neena's hand and waddled off before anyone else could talk her out of it.

"I'm overwhelmed." Alicia simply stared at the two large bags of items we hoped would make things easier for her. "Everyone has been so nice, but I feel like I'm in another world."

We'd followed her to a private waiting room nearby since we weren't allowed in Albert's room. Huddled in a patterned chair with wooden arms, knees drawn up to her chest, Alicia looked like a child.

"Has the doctor spoken to you today?" I pressed gently.

"Just to say the tests showed improvement, but I think everyone's worried. More doctors keep coming in. Some of them talk to me, some of them just look at whatever's on the computer where they keep his information, and then they leave again. They want me to keep talking to him, and I do, but he's not responding any differently today than he did yesterday."

Dropping her head on her knees, Alicia sobbed while I rubbed her back gently. When she spoke again, her voice was muffled. "They think I don't hear them talking or that I don't understand, but I do. Most people never come out of it if they've been in a coma this long. Dr. Maron says he'll do another scan today, and he tries to seem positive. Dad's been breathing on his own since the first week. He opens his eyes sometimes, and his motor response is good —whatever that means. Then the doctor says things about intracranial pressure and Glasgow scales and stuff that Aunt Denise understands. But she's not here, and it all sounds terrifying."

Over Alicia's head, my gaze landed on Patrea. Her mouth set in lines of determination, she nodded to me and quietly left the room. Within minutes, I suspected, someone would show up to give Alicia information in lay terms she could understand.

I wasn't wrong.

Patrea returned with a satisfied look on her face and ushered in the charge nurse, a veritable hulk of a man with a taciturn expression. "We'll leave you to speak privately, and then I know Miss Runyon would like to get back to her father. Alicia, you know how to get in touch if you need anything. Don't hesitate."

There was a threat in her eye that wasn't missed by the nurse, and a promise to Alicia as well.

On the way out, I leaned down to give Alicia a hug and reiterated that I was available at any time, then followed Patrea's stiff-gaited march down the hall.

"Honestly," she fumed. "They're expecting her to advocate for her father, make decisions about his care when they can't be bothered to explain the situation clearly. She's alone for the moment and needs advocacy as much as he does, and I mean to see she gets some help in that department."

When we should have turned left to head toward the parking lot, Patrea turned right instead. Then she stopped and held her keys out toward me. "I'm going to need a few minutes here. You can wait in the car if you want."

Before I could take them, Jacy spoke up. "I'd rather put my mean face on and back you up if that's okay."

"Same goes." Unlike Jacy, Neena could look intimidating when she tried.

I waved off the keys. "I'm in."

We probably didn't manage the perfect wind-in-the-hair, slow-motion turn at the end of the hallway, but it wasn't for lack of effort. That sense of purpose carried us right up to the head of administration's office.

"Miss Heard. Did you have an appointment? I don't remember—" The receptionist frowned.

"No, I was here visiting someone. Is he in?"

"Well, yes, but—"

Patrea didn't listen to the protest. "Thanks, we just need a moment."

Since I'd heard some of her family history over Christmas, I wasn't shocked to hear Patrea call the man behind the desk Uncle Joe.

She introduced us first, and as we took seats, launched right into the reason for busting in on his workday. As succinctly as possible, she laid out Alicia's situation and described our recent experience.

"Someone needs to stand for that girl until her aunt gets back tomorrow. She shouldn't be asked to make decisions for her father without a better understanding of his prognosis and treatment options. Given her age, patient services should be liaising with her father's doctors. She's what?" Patrea turned to me. "Sixteen? Seventeen?"

"Around there. Certainly no older than seventeen. She's still in high school."

Even if she hadn't called him uncle, the family resemblance between Patrea and Joe was easy to see. Older by at least two decades, he shared with his niece the same stubborn set to the jaw, the same brow line lowered over eyes that pierced when they faced one another off across the desk. Her lips might be dyed red with makeup, but they formed the same straight line as his.

He broke first and proved she wasn't the target of his temper. "Budget cuts and vacations mean we're more than short-staffed."

Patrea took pity. "Authorize the staff to talk to me, and I'll stay with her. There's an aunt—the father's sister—coming in from St. Louis tomorrow, but things are happening now. Alicia shouldn't be asked to make patient care decisions based on information that's too technical for her to fully understand. No one should."

"No." Joe held up a hand to stop the tirade before it got fully underway. "They shouldn't. It's not a perfect system, and I'm sorry this girl fell through the cracks."

I'd seen Patrea in crusader mode enough times to recognize the signs, especially on a face that looked so much like hers. "I'll see to her. You have my word."

Satisfied she'd won, Patrea gave her uncle a smile and thanked him, then left him to his job.

"I guess I didn't need to fire up my stank face. That was ridiculously easy. We could have waited in the car." Jacy shivered at the slap of cold air that chilled her skin as we stepped outside. "I was expecting a battle, but you didn't need us at all."

Patrea scoffed. "Fat lot you know. My cousin's wife had a baby right after Thanksgiving, and if you hadn't been there, Uncle Joe'd have pulled out his phone to give me a slide show of the little tyke for an hour. She's as cute as she can be, but I have a low tolerance for looking at twenty-six nearly identical pictures of any baby sleeping in the same position."

Neena barked out a laugh and nudged Jacy with her hip. "Fair warning, then. In another month, you'd better stay away from this one."

"Oh," Jacy agreed, "I'm totally doing that, and I'm not even sorry. I won't be able to help it."

"Noted," came Patrea's dry response.

"I'm sure you'll do the same when it's your turn." Jacy wasn't above giving Patrea a tweak. "I think you and Chris would make cute babies together."

Patrea paled. "I'm not ... we're not—" she stumbled over the speed of her denial.

"Oh, yes, you are. I have a feel for these things. Ask Everly, she'll tell you."

"She does," I agreed as Patrea's face went from white to pink. "She's hardly ever wrong."

"Never wrong." Jacy mock-glared.

Patrea slid behind the wheel but didn't make a move to start the car. "It's too soon to have these feelings. I barely know the man. It's not right."

Neena let out an indelicate snort. "You know him well enough to stay at his house for a week. I'd say that's a start, and who makes the rules about how long it takes to fall for someone?"

With a hint of her former humor, Patrea turned to me, and we spoke simultaneously, "Hallmark."

Patrea started the car and pulled out of the parking lot. "Doesn't matter," she said, "I'm back to work tomorrow, and I'm sure that will be the end of whatever this was. A nice holiday fling or one-night stand that went on a little too long. I'm not the settle-down type, and I can't see him pursuing me once I'm back in my own place."

I reminded her she hadn't thought she was the holiday romance type, either. "Don't put limits on yourself. It's not all or nothing, you know. And you don't have to decide anything today. You live an hour apart. In Maine, we call that just down the road."

"An hour or a world away, it's all the same," Patrea muttered.

CHAPTER EIGHT

"Right there. Turn right. Right there." Reva stabbed a lethally-red tipped finger toward the storage facility with huge signs I couldn't have missed if I tried.

"I see it. Which unit?"

"It's one of the big ones on the back side. 209. Just go around to the left."

"You really didn't need me for this, you know." I could have slept another half hour at least.

"So you've said, but you wouldn't want me to come here by myself, would you? A woman alone on this side of town. It's like sending me into the wolves' den wearing a sheep costume."

A night at the Bide-A-Way hadn't made a dent in Reva's mood. She was still acting as if we'd had a minor tiff, and she could win me over with a girl's day out. Even if I had any interest in restoring our relationship, digging around in a sub-zero storage area for a box of her unmentionables wasn't on my list of bonding activities.

I rolled my eyes and sighed. Nestled in the nicest of suburbs, not even three blocks from the home she'd shared with my ex, Reva wasn't in any danger. Well, that wasn't true, she was, she just didn't know about my desperate desire to throttle the life out of her. And if she didn't shut up, I might give in to temptation.

"It's that one. 209. Do you see it? 209."

"I see it." I swear I wasn't thinking it was an excellent place to hide the body, or not seriously anyway, as I rolled to a stop in front of the only door on the narrow end of the long building.

"You have the key, right?"

"Sure do." Reva dug in her purse and came up with a lone key on a ring. "Come on."

Shaking my head, I said, "I'll wait here."

"You have to help me. It's freezing, and it will take forever to find my boxes if you don't." Reva eyed the back seat. "Good thing you have such a big car."

"It is, isn't it." My jaw clenched. Whether she intended to or not, Reva played on every one of my raw nerves. I sighed but slid out of the warm car. Every inch of skin exposed to the chilled air went stiff with cold. I fumbled for my gloves but only came up with the left one. Great, I didn't need the fingers on my dominant hand for anything. Internally, I cursed Reva's very existence.

You're a gullible fool, Everly Dupree, and she's taking advantage of you ... again.

"This will go much faster if you help. I'll take the left side, you take the right. I'm looking for three boxes about this big." She held up her hands—which, of course, were gloved just to make me feel like more of an idiot for losing one of mine—at about the width of a smaller packing box, gestured to show the height as well. "With my name on them."

While I indulged in a bout of mental name-calling, Reva turned sideways and held up her arms.

"I can't get the key with my gloves on." I ran my tongue across my teeth and swallowed the urge to tell her exactly what she could do with the key as she arched a brow at me, expecting me to take it out of her pocket. When I just looked at her, she rolled her eyes. "We're going to freeze to death because you hate me. Really?"

"Fine." I reached in for the key and allowed myself to appreciate the momentary warmth, then turned and fitted it into the lock.

Without waiting for her to suggest it, I grabbed the door handle and yanked up. The aluminum door was lighter than it looked for its size because it went up like it rode on greased wheels.

Easily fifteen feet wide, the unit was nearly double as deep, with boxes and furniture piled mostly in the center to leave a narrow aisle down either side for easier access.

Feeling just contrary enough to stand in the cold and not help even if it took longer, I stepped back outside as she marched toward the left, and in about two seconds, located one of the boxes she'd come there to find. "Get a move on. I'm freezing, and I don't want to be here all day."

We'd been something that resembled friends to one another, and it wasn't difficult to imagine recent events had altered the way I now viewed Reva. That had to be the reason she now came off like a self-centered child. Or had she acted that way all along? I couldn't trust my memory or my recent experience with her to tell the truth.

For a minute or two, I stood with my bare hand tucked up under my other arm and watched with defiance. *Don't be an idiot*, I told myself. It would be warmer inside the unit. I didn't have to search for boxes, but I could get out of the light breeze.

Except it wasn't a bit warmer inside. Sighing again, I gave in. The faster we got this done, the better.

I made it less than halfway down the length of the room before my stomach tried to exit my body through my mouth. Something was wrong. Very, very wrong.

"Found one."

I went back toward the doors and followed the sound of Reva's voice until I found her.

"You need to get out of here. I have a really bad feeling. Hurry up now." I didn't wait for a response and took her by the arm to drag both Reva and her box out of the unit.

"What is wrong with you?" She yanked her arm away and stomped over to the car to deposit the box on the back seat. "Stop trying to knock me down."

"Shush." I waved her back and, ignoring the pang of recognition I got from seeing some of the furniture I'd helped Paul pick out, went back into the storage room. I didn't have to go much farther than I already had.

"Reva, call 9-1-1, right now. Get the police out

here. Tell them there's been an accident. A horrible accident."

All I could see were his legs, but I recognized the shoes. Brown wingtips with fancy leatherwork around the toes. Lawyer shoes.

A wall dropped down inside my head, or I'd have run screaming into the street instead of moving closer to see if there was any hope.

"What's going ..." Reva's question trailed off as she ignored everything I'd told her to do, crowded up behind me, and saw.

Winston Durham wouldn't be defending my ex, or going to court, or looking down his nose at me ever again. Based on the hole in his chest, someone had made sure of that.

Everything in me wanted to cringe, turn away, stop looking, but none of that mattered. The scene was already burned into my brain.

When Reva burst into tears, I asked, "Did you call the police?"

"I—" her mouth worked, but the only sound that came out was a low scream that went on until I realized this was Reva's version of hysterics and did what I'd only ever seen done on TV. I slapped her—none too gently—to snap her out of it. At any other time, I might have taken some small and petty pleasure from the act, but at that moment, I was too numb to care.

"Did you call the police?" I repeated, but she didn't answer, so I pulled my phone from my jacket pocket and did the deed myself.

"You knew." Reva pulled herself together enough to point a shaky finger at me. "You brought me here because you knew Winston was dead."

If I'd slapped her then, I definitely would have enjoyed it. "Have you gone completely bonkers? You dragged me here, remember? If anyone knew he was here, it was you."

"How could I possibly know Winston would pick my storage unit to commit suicide?"

Ridiculous.

"It's not suicide. There's no gun."

"This is all your fault." Apparently, I'd slapped the fake attempt to be friends right off of her. When she took it up to a shriek, Reva's voice could cut glass. And cause instant headaches. Or maybe that came from trying to follow the twisted path of her logic.

"I haven't seen Winston since the day I found you and Paul doing the nasty, and that was fine with me." On a day that was already right up there in my top three worst—losing Grammie Dupree and my aunt took the highest spots—Winston had leveled the misery up a notch. "In fact, I'd have had a perfectly happy life if I hadn't had to lay eyes on any of the three of you again."

Ignoring the dig, Reva stared at Winston's body as if she finally understood what she was seeing. Her face paled, and her eyes went glassy.

"Go out now, Reva. You don't need to see him like this. Go sit in the car, and I'll wait here for the police. I'll stay where you can see me, okay?"

I wanted a closer look at the body.

Sobbing, Reva obeyed.

Alone with Winston, a chill that was more than merely the cold of the unheated space crept into my bones. Reva might not be the only one to wonder if I'd had enough and done away with one of the men responsible for forging documents that reduced my divorce settlement to nothing. Not that I cared about the money. If I had, I wouldn't have signed the agreement when Paul asked me to. Besides, I'd stepped up, made a life without him, and considered myself better for the experience.

No matter how it looked from the outside, I didn't wish Winston dead. I knew that as I stood and looked down at him and wondered who had.

More accurately, I wondered if Paul was capable of murder. Had he killed and then fled? Was that why Reva was currently staring out my car window?

Operating solely on instinct, I scanned the scene again, noted the pooling blood under his body, the trail of red leading deeper into the middle of the unit. Using my phone as a flashlight, I picked out another, smaller puddle of blood shining darkly, smears of red on the open file boxes, and a scatter of papers.

Winston hadn't died fast or easy. It looked like he tried to get to the door but only made it a few feet before slumping down against the stack of boxes where I'd found him.

A shudder ran through me, but I slipped my phone back in my pocket as the sound of sirens grew louder and went out to greet the authorities.

In the car, her eyes haunted and red-rimmed in her pale face, Reva watched me as I did what needed to be done. The image of her tangled in my sheets, smirking up at me from the shelter of my husband's arms, was one I'd carried for months. Now, I had another to replace it.

"Ma'am." An insistent voice broke my reverie. "You reported a crime." He identified himself as a detective, but his name flew out of my head right after he said it.

"Yes, I'm sorry. He's in there." I pointed toward the storage room. "His name is Winston Durham. Someone killed him." I would have followed the detective to the scene of the crime, but a younger female officer laid a hand on my arm and stopped me.

"Ma'am, I'm Officer Jody Bassett. Do you think you could tell me what happened?"

Below the brim of her hat, Officer Bassett's green eyes missed little.

"I'm Everly Dupree." I spelled it for her while she wrote it down. "And that man in there is Winston Durham. He's my ex-husband's attorney."

"And is this your storage unit?"

"No, it's hers." I pointed to Reva and gave her full name. "She's been dating my ex-husband since we split up." I let out a short, derisive laugh. "Since before that, if you want to get technical. Anyway, the important thing is she and my ex were staying in a hotel after selling our ... his house, but he took off, and since he'd been paying for the room, when he stopped, she had to leave."

"Were they fighting?"

I shrugged. "She says not, but you'll have to ask her. I wouldn't even know that much if she hadn't landed on my doorstep, begging for a place to stay."

Jody Bassett's eyebrows shot up. "And you took her in?"

"No, but I found her a place to stay, and that somehow led to this."

"Do you know if the attorney had a key to the storage unit?"

"Again, you'll have to ask her. All I really know is that she was out of clean underwear, and now, this."

I waved a hand back toward the unit, and in my slightly befuddled state, I knew I wasn't making a whole lot of sense.

"I'm sorry, I'm a little shaken by all this."

"That's understandable." Officer Bassett seemed sympathetic. "And when you arrived, can you tell me what happened?"

"We went in. Reva found one of the boxes she was looking for right away, and then we found him." Because I didn't want to hide possibly relevant information, I gave her the abridged version of Winston's part in my divorce, which led to the story of Paul and the misappropriation of funds, the FBI. Even keeping the recitation of my downfall as brief as I could, it took a minute.

"I'm familiar with the case," was all she said on the subject, and then, "I'll need to talk to Ms. McKinnon."

"Yeah, good luck with that. She's convinced I'm to blame," I said bitterly.

Officer Bassett spoke as a woman now, and not just as a police officer. "I can't tell if you're the nicest woman in the world or the dumbest."

I know I probably should have been offended by her candor, but since I agreed with her, there didn't seem to be much point. By then, I was shaking with cold, so when Bassett suggested I go sit in my warm car, I didn't argue.

"Ms. McKinnon." She tapped on the window to get Reva's attention as I circled toward the driver's seat.

Reva rolled down the window and verified the information pretty much as I'd given it. I listened carefully when Jody asked if Winston had a key to the unit.

"Maybe." Sniffs and tears punctuated every word. "I suppose Winston could have been sent here to find something. There were papers and things in some of the boxes. This is going to devastate my Paulie-poo. They were like brothers. Always talking on the phone and hanging out. I feel like I've lost my brother-in-law." And she was milking it for all it was worth and not earning any points with me.

Still, she'd come looking for Paul at my house. I smelled the distinct whiff of BS, and don't even get me started on Paulie-poo.

Did she call him that to his face? Did he like it? Maybe he preferred a woman who simpered and talked baby talk to him, but that woman would never have been me. Whether she knew it or not, Reva had done me a huge favor. Because that was the moment when I finally said goodbye to Paul and all that we'd been to each other.

CHAPTER NINE

After taking down both our current addresses—I had to give Reva's since she barely remembered the name of the motel, much less its location—Officer Bassett told us we could go home, but cautioned us to remain available in case there were more questions. I sensed from her tone it wasn't a matter of if, but of when.

"Go back," Reva ordered two lights before we would have turned onto the highway. "We have to go back."

"Why?" I slowed down in case she had a valid reason.

"I still need my things. We have to go back for my things."

How dumb was she?

"They're not going to let you take anything else out of that storage room now. It's a crime scene."

"Oh, probably not." She popped her seatbelt off

and spun in the seat to poke at the one box that had managed to make it into the car. "At least I got more clothes."

Reva pulled out her phone, let her fingers fly over the screen as I turned onto the highway. If Paul and Winston were "like brothers," I doubted he'd appreciate learning of Winston's death via text. But his needs were no longer my concern.

"Is there anyone I can call for you? Your parents? Other family?" Funny that after being friends for several years, I knew so little about her. Enough to know her taste in purses and what kinds of movies she liked, but nothing of her family.

"Just take me back to that motel room from throwback hell and leave me there. I want to be alone."

She wasn't the only one, but I was curious enough to push a little.

"Did you and Paul have a fight?"

Reva folded her arms on her chest. "Oh, you'd love that, wouldn't you?"

An hour before, if she'd said yes, I'd have gloated. Probably because I would have been too busy thinking nasty thoughts to hear the forlorn note in her voice. Or if I did, I'd have gloated more.

Seeing death up close and personal—again—put all the pettiness into perspective.

"I really am sorry about Winston, and that you and Paul seem to have split. I think you made him happy in a way I never did."

Mentally letting Paul go had gone some way toward setting me free, and I told myself there was nothing to be gained by carrying on our feud. Since Amber hadn't popped up with a weather report that included hell freezing over, I wasn't inviting Reva to stay with me, but I didn't have the energy to fight anymore, either.

But it wasn't only up to me, and Reva seemed perfectly happy to let silence stand between us, so I drove back to Mooselick River and pulled up in front of her room at the Bide-A-Way.

"Are you sure there's no one I can call? You shouldn't be alone with all that's happening."

"That's something I'll have to get used to, isn't it?" Reva slammed the car door hard enough the hinges creaked.

"If that's the way you feel," I muttered as I put old Sally in reverse. When I turned to make sure the way behind me was clear, I saw the box she'd left in the back seat. Sighing, I put the car back in park and carried the box toward her door.

I knocked and listened to what sounded like an angry she-bear growling and throwing chairs around. Leaving Reva to her tantrum, I set the box down and left. She'd find it when she went out later to eat … using the money she'd borrowed from me earlier in the day.

Way to start the year off with a bang, I thought as I yanked the car door open. I should have noticed that my windows were fogged up. I should have felt the fetid chill, seen the plume of my breath even with the heat on.

"You could have been nicer to her."

I'd seen none of the signs, but the fact that Winston was sitting in the back seat didn't surprise me in the least.

"Screw you." Okay, maybe I'd let go of my animosity toward Paul, and a little bit toward Reva, but Winston was still on my list.

"Must you act like a child?" The man did judgmental better than anyone I'd ever met.

Finally, I turned to face him, and, in tones colder than a ghost, said, "Get out of my car. Get out of my life."

He picked a speck of lint off his lapel—mind-blowing, right? Then he had the nerve to roll his ghost eyes at me. "You're going to help me. You know it, I know it. What's the use in arguing?"

My response? Totally adult and balanced. I turned the radio on and cranked up the tunes loud enough to drown him out. Then, I put the car in reverse, stepped on the gas, and whipped the wheel to spin the car out of the space.

Thank you, Sally, I thought, for not being a gutless wonder. As soon as I hit the main road, I opened her up a little. By the time I slowed for the last curve heading into town, he was gone.

"Good riddance," I shouted into the warming air. "And don't come back."

What grief I'd allowed to creep into my emotional well-being had good and truly dissipated. A mark in the plus column. Or was it? I should feel grief at the brutal murder of someone I'd known. That's how decent people work, and I considered myself a decent person. Winston had been a jerk, but he hadn't deserved to die—and that was as close to grief as I could get. Maybe if he'd gone into the light without bothering me, I'd have had a little more compassion, but no. He had to come slithering around with his ghost self in my car.

I didn't want to help him, but he wouldn't give me a choice. Him having all the power and leaving me with none didn't seem fair.

The time had come to get an expert opinion on my haunting situation.

CHAPTER TEN

The only psychic medium within a hundred-mile radius that popped up when I searched went by the unlikely name of Madame Zephyr and didn't have a website. Based on the name alone, I formed a mental image of an age-wrinkled woman sitting behind a table covered in a red velvet cloth. Haze of smoke around her, wearing lots of makeup, fingers dripping with rings, several pendants tangled across an ample bosom.

But I had to talk to someone about the hauntings, and she was the nearest option.

"Beggars can't be choosers, right, Molly?"

As usual, Molly didn't answer, but I decided to call first thing Monday for an appointment. Searching the Internet for answers to my ghost problem had only raised more questions. I needed to go to the source, talk to someone with solid experience who could put a label on what was happening in my life.

The decision made, I set my phone on the coffee table in case anyone needed me and popped a relaxing chick flick in the DVD player. Fifteen minutes in, with the dogs cuddled up to me for warmth, two short nights caught up with me. I slid so gently into the dream it seemed like a memory until it didn't.

Slowly at first, disjointed images flashed and faded.

Click. I was lying on my stomach on my grandmother's porch. I felt the wooden slats under me, smelled the dust embedded in the wood, and over that, the freshness of misty summer rain. Drops plopped into the puddle that formed beneath the spot where the porch roof slanted against the shed. I wondered how long and how many storms it had taken for splashes of rainwater to wash away the grass and soil, leaving a shallow basin of tumbled stones.

Click. Wild strawberries tangled in tender grass, and I picked them with red-stained fingers. Three for the bowl, one for my mouth. The dream was so real I tasted the burst of sweet juice on my tongue.

Click. I toed back the kickstand of my bike, settled my foot on the pedal, pushed off with a running hop, and swung my leg over the seat. Peddled like crazy until the speed riffled my hair.

Click. Still peddling, but no longer feeling the delicious sense of abandon.

Click. Hearing the roar, seeing the red-eyed monster coming up in the little mirror mounted on the handlebars.

Click. Steep ditch to the right. No escape there, only the inevitable fall.

Click. Too late. The monster screamed. Or maybe that was me.

"Everly. Wake up."

Amber's voice slammed through my subconscious like a hammer on a nail.

"What?" I peeled one eyelid back to see her face too close for my eyes to focus. The chill of her proximity plumed my breath, made me pull the knit throw up to my chin. "Back off a little. You're giving me brain freeze."

"You were moaning in your sleep, and not in a good way."

My head felt like ten pounds of sludge in a two-pound bag. "There's a good way?"

"Well, duh." Amber demonstrated a few of her best sexy moans, and my face set a record for going from cold to hot. Seeing the spreading stain of pink on my cheeks, Amber rolled her eyes.

"You're such a prude."

"I am not." Then I amended the statement. "At least not by polite standards."

"By any standards. Tell me about your dream."

The nightmare, if you could even call it that, had already begun to fade, leaving behind little more than a jumble of impressions and emotions. "Unimportant."

As I tried to sort through some of the fleeting details, my phone gave off an alert tone I'd never heard before. "That's new."

"What is it?" Too curious, Amber forgot herself, crowded in too close, and accidentally brushed against my arm. I flinched away from the sensations of chilled spider legs crawling across my skin.

"Stay out of my personal space, if you don't mind." Touching ghosts sets off my heebie-jeebies. As soon as Amber backed off, I swiped my phone to bypass the lock screen and saw an alert message.

"It's the security system app." I tapped, and a video began to play.

"What is that?" Amber leaned in again but stayed

just shy of actual contact so she could watch the dance of the strange blobs on the screen.

Squinting, I tilted the phone back and forth. "I'm not sure. It doesn't look like anything I recognize." A dark shape moved around near a larger, lighter blob. "What do you think?"

"I think the camera is out of focus. Is that in real time?"

Not wanting to admit I'd spent more time reading about how to mount the cameras and pair them with the app than how to actually use the system, I shrugged. "The instructions mentioned something about sensitivity, and I think I set it to max. It's probably sending out false positives. Why don't you zip outside, take a quick look around, and if there's nobody trying to scale the fences, I can take another run through the manual tomorrow and tweak the settings."

A short battle played across Amber's features as curiosity fought against the annoyance of being asked to run an errand. Curiosity won. She wasn't gone much more than a minute before popping back in to give the all-clear.

"If there was anything out there before, it's gone now." She hovered over the seat of the wing-back chair to my left, propped her elbow halfway through the armrest, and rested her chin in her hand.

"I thought we were friends." Amber treated me to a thousand-yard stare.

I cocked an eyebrow at her. "If you define friendship as forcing your company on me, then I guess we are."

She waved the truth away. "Whatever. Why, if we're friends and all, did I have to hear about Winston Durham's death from hanging around in the newsroom and not from you?"

"Did we develop mind-to-mind communication skills, and nobody told me? Or is there the ghostly equivalent of two tin cans and a string that I'm supposed to use? I can't tell you things when you're not here."

"Ha, very funny. Except I've been here for ten minutes now, and you never said a word."

"Hey, Amber. Winston Durham's dead. There, are you happy now?" I patted the spot beside me to let Molly know it was okay to come up for a cuddle. While Amber seethed, I made a great spectacle out of petting the dog and telling her what a good girl she was.

"I need details," Amber said.

Holding out, I tortured her a few moments more. "Only if you promise not to give me a hard time over the circumstances."

"Cross my heart and hope to..." She followed through on the action but came up short at the word die. "Um ... well, you get the idea. It's a dumb saying anyway."

So I told her everything.

"He'd better not show up here. This is my turf."

Amber wasn't the only one with a thousand-yard stare. "I believe it's mine, thank you very much."

"Whatever."

We might have gotten into it, but the ringtone I set up for tenants jingled from my phone. I boosted Molly off my lap and checked the caller ID before answering.

"Clyde Stone. I wonder what's wrong now," I sighed. My least favorite tenant, Clyde complained about everything.

Every. Little. Thing.

"Good evening, Clyde. What can I do for you?" I only added *you cantankerous fart* in my head because I wanted to keep my job.

"It's supposed to snow." He sounded shaky.

Whether from age or from an excess of his drink of choice, a very cheap vodka, it was hard to tell.

"Yes, I know." The third big storm of the year promised to be the worst of the bunch. The weather app on my phone had been sending out alerts every few hours with new and worsening predictions. I didn't need Mr. Stone to do the same.

"Well," he sputtered in my ear. "What do you plan to do about it?"

Since I hadn't developed any superpower that would let me fly into the sun and change the weather patterns, I wasn't sure how to answer that question. So, I stuttered. "I ... uh."

"About the generator. It hasn't been tested since the last storm."

Living in a town on the outer edge of the power grid had its challenges. Mooselick River went dark at least a couple of times a year. More if the winter was as bad as this one. Since he rented mostly to the elderly and the younger, baby-making set, Leo Hansen, my boss and Clyde's landlord, made sure each unit had a working generator for back-up power.

"That wasn't much more than a couple of weeks ago. I'm sure the system will work just fine." But even as I offered reassurance, I went to get my boots and pull them on. Things would play out one of two ways. I could ignore Clyde's pointed comment and field several more calls before giving in and going over there. Or I could stop the cycle before it started. It wouldn't take more than ten minutes to test the generator.

"Why don't I just come give it a check for you, though. Then you won't worry so much."

"Hurry up then. I have better things to do than sit up all night waiting on the likes of you."

Apparently, five minutes was Clyde's definition of all night since when I got there, the house was dark, and it looked like he had gone to bed. This wasn't the first time he'd done something similar.

A few minutes ahead of my estimate, I was back home and snuggled down to finish the movie I'd slept through earlier. I hit play just as the phone rang again.

"Oh, Clyde," I said to no one. "You're pushing my buttons."

But it was my mother this time.

"I wanted to call and let you know we're leaving in the morning. There's a storm coming, so we decided to get on the road early." She didn't bother with hello but launched right into the reason for the call.

"You couldn't just stay with David's folks until it's passed? Blue's fine here with me, and the school board will delay the re-opening of the term if we get even half the snow predicted."

"Your father didn't want to wait. We'll be just fine. By all reports, it's a slow-moving storm, so as long as we leave early enough in the morning, we'll manage to stay two or three hours ahead of it. We should be back in Mooselick River before noon."

"Keep me updated on your progress, or I'll worry." She agreed, and just before we ended the call, I remembered the question I wanted to ask. "Oh, do you remember that box of office stuff I had the day I moved in here?"

A short pause.

"I'm not giving back the plant. I practically raised it from the dead, so it's mine."

I rolled my eyes even though I figured she'd use her mom vision and know I did. "I don't want the plant back, you can have it with my blessing, but do you remember there was a yellow envelope in the box?"

"Sure. I left it on the countertop near the stove. Why? Is something wrong?"

Better to keep her in the dark for now since I had no idea what was in the envelope. "No. I just remembered it and wondered where it went. I'll check with Jacy. She probably put it away for safe-keeping and then forgot to tell me where."

Or, I'd just hunt the thing down myself. How hard could it be to find one errant envelope?

In a house the size of mine, maybe not so easy, but then, I'd settled mostly into the downstairs rooms, so the place seemed smaller to me than it actually was until the heating bills came in.

Since there was no sense in turning the movie back on, I began my search in the kitchen. Another quick look through the drawers and cabinets turned up nothing more interesting than an extra wire for the cheese slicer and, inexplicably, the missing candlestick from the game of Clue.

One room down, far too many to go.

With that cheery thought in my head, I called it a night and hoped I wouldn't see Winston's corpse in my dreams.

hree texts came in while I watched the dogs race around under white sky the next morning

MOM: *Left an hour later than planned. No snow yet. All good.*

Patrea: *Have you heard about Durham? Call me when you finally deign to crawl out of bed.*

Alicia: *More progress today. A nice man named Joe is helping me understand what's happening. Aunt Denise got a flight out and arrived early this morning. For the first time since the attack, I think he's going to be okay.*

Over breakfast, I responded to all of them while Amber gave me her version of the morning news. My parents could learn about Winston's death once they were home, no sense adding worry to their trip, and I told Patrea I'd heard, and I'd talk to her after work.

She wasn't going to be happy about my part in finding the body. Mostly because I hadn't called her right after it happened. But I'd needed some time to process, and since there was nothing she could do, I wanted to let her have her last night of vacation with Chris unmarred with my problems.

As expected, there was media speculation about Winston's death, but the incoming storm gave him competition for the biggest news story of the day. Shock of shocks, my name wasn't mentioned, nor was Reva's. I suspect Officer Bassett kept our names away from the press, and for that, I owed her a basket of muffins or something.

"According to the reports, the police don't have a suspect at this time," Amber said as I stirred honey into my coffee. "So, I guess you're off the hook."

"I was on the hook?"

"Duh. You found the body, and also because of Paul. Who, by the way, was not listed as missing *or* as a person of interest, only *unable to be reached at this time*. That's telling, isn't it?"

"How do you mean?"

"Well." Amber hover-paced from the stove to the sink. "Reva says he took off, but no one has reported him missing. Don't you think that's interesting? I think it means someone knows where he is. Either the skank or his family."

I thought about that for a moment. "I can't

honestly say if Reva's telling the truth or not. I mean, she hid her relationship with Paul from me for months." Her betrayal still burned a little, even though I'd left my feelings for him behind. "She's quite the little actress."

Amber nodded. "And you said she had to use the key to get into the storage unit, which means whoever killed the lawyer had a key, too."

"Or Winston did. Paul might have given him one."

"Maybe. What kind of lock was it?"

I frowned. "I don't know. It looked like a regular lock to me. Does it matter?" Rising, I took my cereal bowl to the sink.

Whipping around, Amber looked at me like I'd lost my marbles. "Of course, it does. If it came from the storage place, they usually only give out two keys, and it's part of the agreement not to make more. But if Paul bought the lock, it could have come with more, or he had some made. You should ask Reva when you see her again."

"The way we left things, I'd be surprised if I do."

Amber quirked a brow. "She's sponging off you, is she not? Trust me, you'll hear from her."

I hated to admit it, but Amber was probably right. I also didn't let her goad me into another retelling of the entire incident. I'd spent the previous evening going over and over it with her.

"Check back with me later, and see if your prediction was right. For now, I have to get to work, and I honestly need a break from talk of murder."

One of my job duties involved picking up some of the rent checks on the first—or, in this case, the third—of the month. At first, rent day had been my least favorite part of the job. But when I realized those tenants who never mailed or dropped off their payments were older people who hardly ever had visitors, I began to look forward to the day as much as they did.

"Good morning, Mrs. Crabtree. I hope you won't mind, but I've brought you a little present," I said to my first tenant of the day. Mrs. Crabtree lived on the bottom floor of an older house that, despite Leo having updated the heating system and trying to button up the place with new windows and doors, still had some drafty spots. Among the multitude of Catherine Willowby's things, I'd found a brand-new pair of warm slippers and a handmade quilt that, with the placement of some loops and buttons, could be turned into a toasty cover-up.

"Isn't that just something." The elderly lady turned pink with pleasure, and I stayed for half an hour while she talked about people I'd never met, and speculated on how much snow would come before nightfall.

She limped as she walked me to the door, and then stood looking up at the pewter-and-white sky while I stepped out onto the porch.

"The last time I saw clouds like this was the blizzard of '82. You remember that?"

I had to admit I didn't.

"My knee's been playing me up since half-past six. Them weather people on the TV don't know their elbows from a hole in the ground. You'd think they'd have enough sense to look out the window and see what's what. You'd better get a wiggle on and finish up your rounds before noon if you don't want to get caught in a white-out." Her prediction left me a couple of hours to finish up, but I wasn't worried.

Halfway to my next stop, I got a text from my mom proving Mrs. Crabtree's knee never lied.

—Forecast wrong. Starting to snow earlier than

anticipated. We're being careful, but might be a little later than planned. Still okay, though.

—*Where are you now?*

She named a point a few miles shy of halfway, so a bit more than three hours driving in good weather and some of that through mountainous territory. I took a deep breath to push back the worry, then moved on to the next tenant, and then the next.

Grammie Dupree always said that if you had a list of chores to do, you should make the worst one the first one. Grammie Dupree didn't have to deal with Clyde Stone. I saved him for last.

He met me at the door and waved the rent check in my face.

"It's about time you showed up to check the generator. You want me to pay, you'll take care of business first."

Maintaining eye contact the entire time, I snaked the fluttering check out of his hand, folded it in half, and stuck it in my pocket.

He dropped his eyes before I did. The best way to stop a bully is to stand up to him. There's a fine line between respecting your elders and letting someone walk all over you.

"Please," he said. "Would you check the generator?"

"Of course."

Clyde stepped back to let me in and followed me through the house to the power panel. He didn't have a lot of furniture, and what he did have looked ancient. The house echoed around him, and as much as I didn't like him most of the time, I felt sorry for Clyde.

"All the units are set to run for a few minutes on Sundays just to make sure everything is working correctly. Leo and I both receive an alert if they don't." I had reminded Clyde of this before, but I flicked the main switch anyway—something he could have done himself—and the generator rumbled to life. "See, everything's working fine."

My smile felt forced. "Is there anything else I can do for you?"

"Matter of fact, there is." He banged his cane on the floor. "I need some things from the grocery store." Clyde pulled a piece of folded paper out of his shirt pocket, handed it to me, then reached for his wallet while I yanked my lower jaw back up.

"I didn't mean—" I began to talk my way out of errand duty, then thought better of it. With the flu still raging through town, it might be best for him to stay out of the grocery store. No sense in costing Leo a tenant because I didn't care much for Clyde's attitude. He was my last stop of the day, and there were a few things I could pick up for myself. It wouldn't take long to come back around this way, so saying no would just be churlish.

"'Preciate it." He dug out his wallet, peeled off a couple of tens, and handed them to me. "That oughta cover it. Hurry and get back before that white crap starts to pile up."

I left, and as I pulled my car door shut, the first flakes drifted across my windshield. It was quarter to noon.

At the grocery store, the bread aisle looked like a hurricane had hit. Only a few loaves sprawled across the shelves.

"Ain't much milk left, either." A man I didn't know brushed past me to grab all but one of the remaining loaves. "Better get a gallon or two before they're gone."

I wouldn't go through two gallons of milk if the storm lasted a week, but Clyde had bread and a quart of milk on his list, so I took the last loaf and headed toward the coolers. I wasn't in the store more than ten minutes, but when I went back out, a steady curtain of white had begun to fall.

By the time I dropped the rent checks at the bank and turned down Tulip to deliver Clyde's groceries—which included two bottles of rotgut vodka—a sloppy mix of snow and ice had built up at the edges of my windshield and crusted along my wiper blades. Their swish-swish noise nearly hypnotized me, which is why my heart skipped a beat when, through the whirling snow, I thought I saw a girl pushing her bicycle along the snowy edge of the street.

With a hit of adrenaline coursing through my veins, I jammed my foot down a little too hard on the brakes. Old Sally slid right past Clyde's place, and when I finally coaxed her to a stop so I could look for the girl, there was no sign of her. Nor, when I made my way toward the front steps, was there a single footprint or tire track in the street other than my own. She must have gone inside while I was getting the car under control.

Clyde gave me a hard time about how long I'd been gone, and how much the bread had cost.

"I'm on a fixed income. I can't afford that fancy stuff with all the grains and such. Why didn't you get plain old store brand?"

"You're lucky to have any, given the way the shelves were picked clean."

It took longer to drive home than it would have taken to walk, and I didn't see the girl or her bike again, but I did see the white van in the church parking lot.

My mother hadn't responded, nor did she when I sent another text asking for an update. When I tried to call, it went straight to voice mail, so I left a message.

"It's me. Call me back. I'm beginning to worry."

Next, I called Leo.

"Checks are in the bank, and everyone seems to be settled in for the storm." We talked shop for a few minutes, then he cleared his throat somewhat ominously.

"I had a phone call about you that I find concerning."

"From one of the tenants?" I tried to think who might have a problem that I hadn't handled already and came up empty.

"No."

Up until the moment he'd serenaded his longtime crush in the middle of her restaurant, most people in town had considered Leo something of a wimp. Nice enough guy—no one ever said different—but unassuming to a fault. The kind who avoided confrontation, and so when he hemmed and hawed, I knew whatever he had to say was making him uncomfortable.

"If you were planning to quit, you'd give me notice, right?" He finally said.

"Of course, I would." Was I getting fired? "But I'm not planning to quit. I really like this job, and I think I'm pretty good at it. Did someone complain?"

Seeming more comfortable, he said, "I got a call from someone saying they were reaching out on behalf of a potential employer and asked a lot of questions about you. Odd questions, too. Not ones I would ask if I was planning to hire someone."

Considering my job interview had consisted of him telling me I should take over from my murdered former employer, I wasn't sure what Leo considered proper interviewing etiquette. I didn't think he'd done a lot of hiring or firing before me, but I'd also had a few headhunters come calling during my time working for the Hastings family, and this could be another.

"Well, don't worry, I'm not planning on getting another job. I like the one I have."

Who wouldn't? Part-time work, for nearly full-time pay because I was on call twenty-four-seven, and working for a man who went above and beyond as a landlord for his tenants. The only thing I was more thankful for than this job was that Leo hadn't bent the rules when I'd returned to town needing a place to live. If he had allowed me to move in without two week's pay stubs, I'd have become one of his tenants instead of a homeowner.

The planets had aligned for me. I reassured Leo and got him off the phone. My mother still hadn't responded, so I tried calling her again. Then I tried my dad's phone, and David's with the same results. Straight to voice mail. They must be out of range. My mind offered an image of them buried in a snowbank, or worse, teetering on the edge of a cliff.

Three hours later, early darkness filtered down through storm clouds that did half the looming night's work for it, and my parents still hadn't arrived. The dogs had watched me cook to keep busy, and then watched me pace as if the march of the insane human was high entertainment.

I tried to sit. Tried to watch TV but only managed a minute or two before rising to go into the front room and look out the window for the hundredth time. My phone beeped for an incoming email. If I wanted it and the weather held, I had an appointment with Madame Zephyr at one the next day. I responded and confirmed the time, then went back to the kitchen to turn the burner under my pot of stew down to a simmer.

I turned on the maps app on my phone, calculated their route, and made sure the traffic setting was toggled on. It took a while, but by flicking my finger about a million times, I was able to scan the half of the route they'd been on since she'd called. Since every major road in the northeast showed up yellow, it wasn't hard to figure that traffic was running very slow. But I didn't see any crash indicators or areas of red that meant cars weren't moving at all.

When the phone finally rang, it was only Jacy asking for an update.

"I'm sure they're fine, and you know cell service is iffy when there's a heavy storm. You wait and see, they'll be along any minute now."

As much as she meant to be reassuring, her cheerful tone set my nerves twitching, so I snapped at her. And immediately regretted being a jerk.

"I'm sorry, Jace. I didn't mean that."

"Forget it. I already have. Call me the minute you hear anything, though."

I promised I would, and that I'd come by the shop the next day. I hadn't told Jacy or Neena about Winston yet. It could wait until I saw them both at the same time and only had to tell the story once.

When we hung up, I finally gave in, turned off the TV, took a warm throw and the pillows from the sofa, and settled in on the deck of the bay window to keep watch.

It seemed like hours before I saw headlights on the street, but it wasn't more than ten minutes later when my parents' car pulled into my drive.

Blue and I met them at the door. One look at my mother's exhausted face made me swallow the scolding I'd been about to deliver. "Are you okay?" She shrugged off her coat, and uncharacteristically let it fall to the floor.

"I will be in a minute," She half walked, half ran toward the bathroom while my father leaned down to give Blue's ears a welcoming scratch.

"You must be starving." I bent to retrieve her coat and fold it over my arm. "And tired of driving. I made chicken stew."

To keep busy, I'd cooked enough for everyone and

then some. My father looked worse than my mother, and even David's face was gray with fatigue.

"We should probably just take Blue and head on home. Looks like at least a foot already, and we'll have to wallow our way in to get David's truck going so we can plow out the end of the driveway."

"I took care of that for you." Planning ahead helped me get through the hours of worry. "Leo's plow guy has been keeping you cleaned out on his rounds. And I stopped in just before noon to turn up the heat so you wouldn't have to come home to a cold house. Take off your coats, come have a hot meal, then you can go home, put your feet up, and relax."

"Sold." Some of the tension left my father's shoulders. "We'd have been here an hour ago, but we stopped to help a young woman get back on the road."

"Well, you're here now, and that's all that matters."

My mother had taken the time to fix herself up a little, and she looked more like herself when she returned, but before she'd sit down to eat, she reminded David to call his folks and let them know he was safe.

"We didn't get service until we passed the grocery store, and all your texts came in at once."

"I guess that explains the radio silence, then." But she'd reminded me to let Jacy know everyone was safe, which I did while everyone settled in at the table.

Over stew, they described their harrowing trip, and I gave them a downplayed version of the news about Winston.

"Do you think you're a suspect?" David cut a dumpling in half with the side of his spoon.

Patrea and I had discussed the possibility at length, but couldn't come up with a plausible enough motive for the police to take a hard look at me.

"I'm probably on their list, but way down at the bottom. If he'd been killed a few months ago, I might have been higher up, but I had no reason to want Winston dead. Murder investigations take a lot longer in real life than they do on TV, and if the police have questions, they know where to find me. But I'm betting Paul's a more likely suspect than me."

"I worry about you living here alone." Some of the tension lines were back around my mother's eyes.

"I have the security system up and running, and I can set it to send notices to your phone if that will make you feel better, but I'm not scared. Not with Molly around."

Mom made me set up the notices before they left, and I admit I felt better having a backup. With my family safe and sound, I pushed all thoughts of murder out of my head, went to bed early, and slept like the dead until Molly nudged me awake at a reasonable hour the next morning.

CHAPTER TWELVE

Snow crunched under my tires as I pulled down the side street where Madame Zephyr lived in the little town of Oakville.

"Not what I expected," I said to Molly, who sprawled across the back seat. I inspected the tidy yellow house behind the white picket fence. Well, technically behind the tips of the fence, which were the only things showing above drifted snow. "But it's cheerful."

Several times during the two-hour drive, I'd talked myself into and out of turning around. What if she took one look at me and said my ghost problem would only get worse? What if they started popping out of the woodwork wherever I went?

My hand itched to drop the car in reverse and call this a bad idea, but the curtain at the front window twitched back, and I knew she'd seen me sitting there. Now I had to go in.

Molly watched me walk up the steps onto the

front porch and ring the bell next to a small, tasteful sign announcing I was in the right place. My pulse sped up a couple of notches when the door opened almost before the final peal faded to silence.

"Uh, hi," I said to the woman who stood waiting. "I'm here to see—"

"Madame Zephyr." One dark brow arched up over twinkling brown eyes, and a gentle smile teased the corner of a bow-shaped mouth. "Come in, won't you? It's Everly, right? Everly Dupree from Mooselick River."

I stepped past so she could close the door behind me, and she looked out to see Molly scrambling from the back to the front so she could watch from the passenger's seat.

"Is that your dog? What's his name?"

Expecting a dark and smoky den, I wasn't prepared for the interior to be as sunny and bright as the exterior. Better yet, no hint of burning sage perfumed the air.

"Her name's Molly. She loves to ride, so I brought her along. Is that a problem? She's not much of a barker, so she won't bother your neighbors." Now that I was inside, I hoped I wasn't about to be sent packing. Better to get this over with all at once.

"No, it's not a problem at all. I love dogs. You should bring her in so I can meet her properly."

"Don't you have to ask ... um ... Madame Zephyr if it's okay?"

The response came in the form of a sparkling laugh. "This happens all the time. Let me introduce myself. I'm Kathleen Canton, but you can call me Kat. Most everyone does because Madame Zephyr was my grandmother. I only took the name because it meant so much to her."

If she hadn't delivered the bombshell with a wry twist of the lips, I'd have felt like an idiot, but she came across as genuine and humble. I snapped my mouth shut because it had dropped open in surprise, then took her up on the offer to bring Molly inside. I needed a moment to collect my thoughts anyway, and getting the dog would give me that chance.

Talk about mixed emotions and a certain perverse irony in both needing and dreading whatever Kat might say. Still, she seemed kind enough and didn't give off nearly as much of the whackadoo vibe as Momma Wade.

"Sorry, Leandra," I offered the apology to the wind because I felt terrible about how the woman I loved came out in the comparison. "Okay, Molly, let's do this."

Sleek as a seal, the dog bolted for the door when Kat opened it, nearly yanking me off my feet when her leash went taut. Out of self-preservation, I let go when I normally would have spoken sharply and held Molly to her training, and she took the stairs in a single bound.

A quick vision of Kat being bowled over by a chocolate-colored bullet passed before my eyes as I stumbled after the dog knowing it was already too late. I heard the thump of a tail on the floor as I gained the top step.

"Are you all right? I'm so sorry."

Kat laughed. "I'm fine." By some miracle, she was still on her feet with Molly sitting placidly at her side. I closed the door behind me. "She sees, too."

I understood the odd statement without needing explanation.

"She does."

Before I could tell the story of how Molly had come to me, Kat held up a hand for silence. "He charged her with your care before he left, and you with hers."

Deepening in tone, her voice shivered over me,

and in the process of shedding my coat, I pulled it tighter around me instead. Uh oh, I thought, here comes the freaky stuff. And then I felt small for passing judgment on someone for doing the thing I'd come for help with.

As if she read my thoughts, and maybe she had, Kathleen gently but firmly helped me out of my coat and led me to a kitchen that reminded me a bit of my own. Bright colors, patterned kitchenware, and lots of light made the room homey. Kat settled me in a spot at her kitchen table.

"Chamomile and lavender, I think. Do you like tea? I find it so soothing." She kept up a light chatter while she scooped loose tea into a flower-covered pot with a smart little strainer built right in. "Do you trust me?"

"I don't even know you." There was not enough chamomile in the world to stop my stomach from fluttering.

Kat poured hot water into the pot. "But do you trust me? Don't think about it. Let your intuition be your guide. What does your gut say?"

Surprising myself, I said, "Yes. But I don't know why." I let out a breath that took the tension with it.

"Good. Because I only want to help. Now, tell me about your ghosts."

So, I laid out the whole sordid story. I told her about Hudson, and then about Spencer and how I'd come to have Molly in my life. Then there was Nick and Amber and Winston. Finally, I voiced my worst fear.

"I thought I was just the victim of a bizarre set of hauntings because of my connections and proximity to far too many dead bodies, but Amber won't leave, and I think there's a ghost named Felicity hanging around my friend's shop. I felt something the other day, but I can't be certain. What scares me is I never met Felicity, and I wasn't even in the area when she died. So there goes my theory on hauntings."

The tea smelled good, but the way my stomach churned, I wasn't sure I could keep it down. Not that I took more than a sip anyway, because once I'd begun to unload, I couldn't seem to stop talking.

"My grandmother wasn't like yours. Neither of them, actually. I can't remember any mention of seeing ghosts, and Grammie Dupree would have been tickled pink if she could. She wouldn't have kept it a secret. So I can't be a medium, right?"

Kat raised an eyebrow, took a sip of tea, then rose

to retrieve her phone. She tapped out a text and then laid the phone face down on the table. "You could, but I'm not getting the vibe."

There's a bag of whacky in my head sometimes. That's the only explanation I have for why I felt slightly offended by the affirmation of the one thing I'd come there hoping to hear. "I should have brought Amber with me. Then you'd see a vibe."

Except that the minute Amber had heard where I was going, she lit out of my place like her hair was on fire. Probably scared Kat would send her into the light whether she wanted to go or not. I drained my tea—which surprisingly helped settle my stomach—and set the cup back down on its saucer. All my hopes for definitive answers deflated like a pin-poked balloon.

"If that's all there is to say on the matter, I guess I'll get out of your hair. Come, Molly." I pushed back my chair, and the whole room chilled.

"Everly Dupree, you sit right back down in that chair and show this nice young lady some respect."

My grandmother's voice coming out of Kat's mouth sucked the strength right out of my legs, and I wasn't left with any choice in the matter. I didn't trust my knees not to wobble, and I couldn't have stood up if I'd wanted to. I also couldn't think in coherent sentences, much less speak them.

The moment passed before I had a chance to say anything, anyway.

"Grandmothers," Kat said with some acerbity. "Do they ask permission first? No, they just pop up, take over, have their say, and then off they go, without so much as a thank you."

"If that ever happened to me, I'd—" I wasn't sure what I'd do, but I figured peeing my pants might make the top of the list. "You know what? No. I can't do this. No offense, but I don't want to be like you. I mean, you seem nice enough, and you're not a flake or anything, but I can't do that. What you just did. I can't."

I knew I was babbling and saying things that weren't all that nice, but I couldn't seem to stop myself.

"Nope." I shook my head. "You have to help me make it go away. There has to be a way to make it stop. Leandra did once, but then I used that stupid Ouija board, and now I'm screwed, right?"

The doorbell ringing about five times finally cut off the spate of foolishness.

"That'll be the cavalry." She smiled at me on her

way to open the door, which made me feel lower than I already did for making the flake comment, and I vowed to staple my mouth shut before anything stupid came out of it again.

And then I nearly broke that promise when a fairy-like vision in purple appeared before me.

"Hi," the vision said in a voice too deep to match her diminutive size. "I'm Amethyst."

"Uh, I'm Everly."

"I was wondering," Kat said, "if you could take a look at Everly, and tell us what you see."

Amethyst raised an eyebrow dyed a delicate shade of lavender to match the slant of her blunt-cut hair. "Is that okay with you?" She said to me.

I glanced over at Kat, who nodded reassurance, though I wasn't sure precisely for what. "Sure, I guess. Unless looking at me is a euphemism for something weird."

"Weird is in the eye of the beholder." Amethyst's answer inspired no confidence. "All I'm going to do is read your aura." Leandra would have had a field day with this. Maybe I'd make an appointment for her next birthday.

"Okay, do your worst."

But look at me is all she did. First with her head

tilted to the left, then to the right. Then she asked me to stand in front of a blank wall in Kat's reading room, and she looked at me some more. I felt like a bug under a microscope.

Finally, Amethyst said, "Do you mind if I just—" She sounded distracted and began to pluck at the air around me. It might have been my imagination, but I thought I felt little tugs in my body each time she did. A change in tension. The looking and plucking went on for quite some time.

"You're carrying a lot right now, aren't you? Why don't you tell me about it?"

Normally, I would never dump my troubles on a stranger, but then, a stranger isn't usually elbows deep in my aura. I spilled everything to her, much as I had to Kat, only with a lot more detail. Blurted it all out in a long rush that was part rant, part revelation. Everything from finding Paul in bed with Reva to feeling the cold specter of Felicity in the shop to Winston and my complete lack of wanting to help him into the light. I ended up with the worry that I was somehow the catalyst for dead bodies popping up left and right.

Amethyst kept on grooming my aura during the

process, and by the end, I felt husked out and somehow lighter than I had in months.

Until Kat handed me a tissue, I didn't realize I'd been crying. Or that two other women had quietly entered the house and heard at least some part of, if not my entire story.

"I'm sorry," I said to Kat. "You must have had other appointments for the day, and I've gone way over my time. I'll get Molly and get out of your hair right now." I'd nearly forgotten the real reason I'd come, and to be honest, I wasn't even sure I wanted answers anymore. Being haunted wasn't the worst thing that had happened to me over the past few months.

And there's a sentence I never thought I'd say.

"Molly." I glanced around for my dog and started to stand to leave.

"Everly!" Kat must have said my name more than once to get my attention. "Please, don't go. I don't have any appointments besides you today. These are my friends. This is Julie," she pointed toward a pert blonde woman with kind eyes.

"Nice to meet you." I smiled at her halfheartedly.

Then Kat pointed toward a spot on my left, "And that's Gustavia."

I turned to see my dog sprawled across the floor with her head in the lap of a woman with a cheerful face and fashion sense that made it hard to take her in all at once. My brain could only process the chaos in stages.

"Uh, hi." To be fair, I'm sure Gustavia got that reaction a lot. Her attention, though, was all for Molly as she cooed and gave the dog's belly a scratch.

My first good look at her registered a flowing skirt in a wash of blues and greens with a dark, figured pattern overlay. By itself, the filmy skirt wasn't anything unique, but she'd paired it with a hot pink top under a lime green vest that peeked through a confetti of beaded necklaces.

It's not polite to stare. This I know, and yet, I couldn't seem to drag my gaze away from her face, topped as it was by a nest of twisted and braided hair. A literal nest, I mean. Just a small one with a tiny bird perched on the edge and an even smaller crystal egg in the center.

Kat caught me looking and let out a tinkling laugh. "For Gustavia, this is a toned-down look." When my eyebrows shot up, she laughed again. So did Amethyst and Julie.

"I wear only that which gives me joy." Gustavia defended her fashion choices with a grin. "Today seemed like a hatch-y sort of day. I think maybe the universe was telling me I'd be helping someone come out of their shell."

I didn't realize she meant me until she plucked the hairpin with the crystal egg attached to it from her hair and reached up to hand it to me. "With everything you've gone through, it would be easy to close off your heart. Don't do that, okay?"

There was nothing else to do but slide the hairpin into place, and I have to admit, I felt better for being the subject of such kindness. I'd opened up a lot of old wounds during my blurt, and Gustavia reminded me a little of Jacy. Comforting and kind. Put the two of them together, and things might get dangerous. Or at least colorful.

After exchanging meaningful looks, Kat and Amethyst left the room.

"I know what you're going through," Julie said into the silence they left behind. "It wasn't that long ago when I had my little ghostly encounter, but everything turned out well enough for me. I'm sure it will be the same for you."

A spear of hope flared inside of me. "You've seen ghosts?"

Gustavia started to speak, but Julie pointed a finger at her. "No, it's my story. I get to tell it."

"You never let me have any fun." Gustavia's smile belied her words, and she seemed content enough to stay seated on the floor with Molly while I took a seat opposite Julie, who launched into her tale.

"It happened right here," she began. "*Someone* thought a visit to a psychic would be a good engagement gift." The way her eyes cut to Gustavia, I had no trouble figuring out who that someone had been. "My grandmother came through, and it really freaked me out. I thought that was the end of the madness, but later that night, she popped back up at home, and she wasn't alone. She brought my great grandfather with her so he could reveal a family secret that completely turned my life around."

With Gustavia chiming in, Julie spun a story worthy of being made into a book. Or even a series of them. As I listened to them tell me about how the ghosts of Julie's grandparents had guided her through finding the secrets hidden in her house, my ghostly experiences seemed far more commonplace. I asked few questions until the end.

"And that was it? You don't see ghosts anymore?"

"No, that's Kat's specialty—and don't let her fool you with this Madame Zephyr business, she's the real deal. Kat uses her abilities to help police solve cold cases, and she occasionally gets called in on some of the hot ones, too. You can trust her."

Of course, her friends would say that, but I didn't think Julie was lying. I'd have told her so if Kat and Amethyst hadn't returned at that moment. Their solemn faces set my guts jumping again.

"Just tell me if I'm going to be perpetually haunted, okay?" I said. "I'd rather know the worst than keep guessing."

"It's complicated," Kat said. "Those with the gift of clairvoyance, or clear sight, can see spirits who have fully transitioned. Ghosts—or spirits who have not crossed over—can and often do reveal themselves to the sightless, but it costs them a lot of energy to overcome the barrier between this world and the next. This is where the idea of ghosts being filmy and white comes in."

"Like in the movies." Gustavia fidgeted with one of the many rings she wore.

"Okay," I drew the word out long. "And by crossing over, you mean going into the light?"

Kat nodded her encouragement. "That's exactly right."

I was beginning to understand. Or I hoped I was. "Once they've gone into the light, I never see them again, but the ones I do see don't look like movie ghosts at all. They look like everyone else with maybe a little blur around the edges, and they hover a little sometimes. Plus, they're creepy to touch." I shivered just thinking about it.

"Seeing that clearly is normally a sign of someone with a high degree of ability."

"Well, you know, I always say if you're going to do something, you should commit to it a hundred percent." I let out some of my nerves as sarcasm. "Maybe I should make a conscious effort to half-ass a few things, though. Might make my life easier."

Gustavia snorted indelicately. "I like you. You're funny."

She thought I was joking. I wasn't so sure I was.

Kat had ended her sentence in such a way I knew there was a but coming.

"But—" I prompted.

"But as far as I can tell, you weren't born with enough of the gift of sight to show up as even a blip on my radar."

"What does that mean?" Gustavia prompted. "I mean, I know someone can be born with the ability, but isn't it possible to develop a sixth sense later in life?"

Amethyst and Kat exchanged a look, but Kat answered readily. "Many people are born sensitive, but for one reason or another, some are able to block their own abilities for a period of time. That didn't work out so well for me, but others manage with more success. Even if they do start to acknowledge their gift later in life, they had it all along."

While that fact was interesting, it didn't answer the question, and I knew there was yet another *but* coming.

"But the chances of someone who has no inherent talent suddenly becoming a full sensitive," Amethyst said and nodded toward me, "I would say happens only under extenuating circumstances."

Kat took over the narrative. "Sometimes, a near-death experience will open the third eye, and there are certain drugs that can do the same. At least temporarily. I don't recommend either of those things, and we already know that's not what happened with you."

"No," I shook my head. "It's not."

Her mouth settling into a straight line, Amethyst waved a finger at me. "Your friend shouldn't have been messing with things she doesn't understand."

"Leandra meant well." I defended the woman who was like a second mother to me, even though she'd brought a world of annoyance into my life. "All she did was rub some oil and ashes on my forehead. She was trying to help."

"I don't understand how ashes and oil could turn Everly into a medium." Looking intrigued, Gustavia gently slid out from under my sleeping dog to take a seat on the sofa. "Do you remember exactly what it was she used?"

"No." Julie laughed and held up a hand. "Don't answer that. If you do, she'll start dousing herself with oil and rolling around in the fireplace. Gustavia has enough talents already. She doesn't need to start taking in stray ghosts. She'd end up with a houseful."

Eyes flashing, Gustavia opened her mouth to offer a retort, then paused, pursed her lips, and twisted them to the side. "I hate to say it, but you're probably right. I'd better leave the ghost wrangling to the professionals. I'd still like to know how it worked, though."

"That's easy enough." Amethyst left the room to return with a bottle of cooking oil in one hand and a frosted glass candle holder minus the candle.

"Imagine this glass was covering your eye. You might see different shades of light through it, maybe even a shadow or two, but mostly, you'll see just the white glass." She drizzled oil on the frosted surface and used her fingers to rub it around. "But just do this," when she held it up again, the frosted surface had turned clear enough to see through. "And look what happens."

Out of reflex, my fingers found the spot on my forehead where Leandra had applied the oils. "If it's that simple, anyone could do it."

Having settled next to me, Kat reached over to gently squeeze my other hand. "It's not, actually."

"No," Amethyst said. "You experienced the perfect storm. There was a newly-minted ghost already attached to you, and then when your friend misheard her spirit guides, she blended his energy with yours, added an amplifier to the oils, and had just enough natural healing power to open up a one-way channel right to your third eye. As a result, she's altered your aura beyond my ability to repair it, and while she might not have meant you any harm, she certainly hasn't done you any favors."

She asked a lot of questions, made me go over the details from finding Hudson's body to when his ghost appeared, and everything she heard strengthened her supposition.

Because of the way he'd died, Hudson hadn't crossed into the light, and since I'd been the one to find him, he'd latched his energy onto mine in the hope of finding someone who could help him.

It had been his distress more than mine that Leandra had sensed that day when she'd smeared on the oil and ashes, but I was still the one who paid the price for her meddling. She'd left me with a ghost problem and a damaged aura.

"You can't blame it all on her, though, because she did manage to fix her mistake temporarily. I'm the one who picked the aura scab by using the Ouija board. But I didn't have a choice. My friend was in danger, and now, I guess I'm a medium." Since I still needed clarity on the finer points of how this all worked, I let my voice go up a little to make the statement almost a question.

"Not quite." Kat laughed, presumably at the dread in my tone, though I hadn't meant any offense.

"Then what am I?"

Kat and Amethyst exchanged another look. "Ghost whisperer?" Amethyst offered.

"More like a ghost magnet," Kat corrected.

Great.

CHAPTER THIRTEEN

"That was quite the trip, wasn't it?" I said to Molly as we passed the sign welcoming us back to Mooselick River. As always, Molly had no opinion.

Amber did, and I jumped when she appeared in the seat next to me. "Waste of time if you ask me."

"Really? Why's that?"

"Nothing changed, did it? You still see ghosts; I'm living proof of that."

"Living?" I snorted. "Not quite."

"Fine, I'm dead proof. Nitpick the terminology if you must, but I'm here, and I assume Winston's whirling around in the ether somewhere waiting to take another crack at you."

"I suppose you're right." Talking to Kat and her friends had eased my mind more than Amber could have done, but I didn't bother telling her that. She wouldn't appreciate the comparison and was likely to drop the temperature inside the car by twenty degrees if I annoyed her.

"But I still want to see if Felicity is really hanging around the shop. She must have used a lot of energy trying to contact me, given our tenuous connection." According to Amethyst, Nick had probably drawn Felicity's attention to me and served as some sort of conduit. If she appeared, I hoped to ask her if that had been the case.

"I'll help."

Whoops. I'd walked right into that one, and by the time I'd parked in the darkened lot behind Curated Collections, I hadn't come up with a graceful way to walk back out of it, so I dug out my spare key.

On the first day of Kindergarten, Jacy had walked up to me, taken my hand, and declared she would be my friend forever. A prediction that had proved correct so far, and yet, I hadn't known about her deep desire to own a second-hand shop.

She'd kept that one to herself until the day we'd found Catherine Willowby's secret treasure trove in the addition tacked onto the back of my house. It seemed the two women shared a passion for collecting, only Catherine had less interest in reselling than in creating pieces of art out of old things.

Having read some of Catherine's diaries since then, I'd come to understand that in exploring her artistic whims, she was looking for a balm to soothe an aching loss. While Paul hadn't been the kind of husband to me that Basil had been to Catherine, I identified with her need to recreate a sense of self after his death. Jacy identified with her need to take something old and give it new life.

Since then, I'd been slowly clearing out the volume of things in those rooms and supplying the shop with furniture, old glass, and anything else that Jacy thought she could sell. As far as I was concerned, we had a win/win situation going. I made a little extra money, Jacy and Neena had plenty of stock, and eventually, I'd send enough to make a dent in the sheer volume of stuff. My contribution, and the fact that I filled in for Jacy or Neena when they needed a day off, made me feel like I had a stake in the store.

"Felicity!" I felt a little foolish talking to empty space. "If you're here, I'd like us to talk. I think I might be able to help you." Dead quiet. "Felicity?"

I supposed silence was its own answer.

"Okay, I guess you don't want my help."

Static electricity crept along my skin, sending pinprick shocks up and down my arms, the sensation teasing the little hairs until they stood at attention. I moved behind the counter and took a seat on the stool Jacy routinely used when her ankles swelled from standing.

"Show yourself." I should have added please to the end because my request came off more like an order, and Felicity wasn't having any of it. One of the round racks began to whirl. Slowly at first, then faster. Jeans whizzed and spun, the speed lifting them higher, arcing them wider, slapping them against other racks of clothing.

The air vibrated. This was probably how the term poltergeist came to be.

"That's quite a show." I kept my cool, but with some difficulty. Still, my reaction was a lot better than it had been when Hudson popped up the first time. My cool lasted right up until a cut-glass candy dish—one from Catherine's collection—flew off a shelf and whipped past my ear so close the wind from it blew my hair in my eyes.

I won't deny I considered huddling under the counter, but I'm not proud of it. I caught the next thing she tossed at me and channeled my mother's stern tones. "That is enough!" I roared and then blinked in the near silence with the only noise coming from the rack that still revolved, but more slowly now.

"I said I was here to help you, but I will rethink the offer if this is how you're going to behave."

From the farthest corner of the store, I heard a muffled, "Sorry."

Finally, we had real contact.

Maybe my knees shook a little as I crossed the room, but I tried not to let my fear show in my outward appearance. For one, I didn't want a repeat of the past few minutes, and for two, I wanted her to see she could trust me.

I found Felicity sitting on the floor, her head resting on her drawn-up knees and her body shaking with pent-up fear or frustration. Oftentimes, the two appear the same.

"Aw, honey." I wished I could put an arm around her and offer a comforting hug. All I could do was try the verbal version. "I know this is scary." And not just for her. "But it's going to be okay."

"How?" Her head popped up, and I got my first look at my newest visitor from beyond the grave. Dark hair framed deep-set eyes. I couldn't help but think she looked like her father—the man who had attacked my father at Halloween. "Exactly how is this okay? No one but you can hear me. My father and mother are gone, and I'm stuck in this—" she grimaced, waved a hand. "Place."

"Do you remember what happened to you?" I had to ask. "You know you're—"

"Dead? Yeah, I got that. I'm not stupid."

The bravado lasted about three more seconds before Felicity's body quivered. "What's going to happen to me?"

Torn between wanting to provide comfort and telling the truth, I said, "I don't know. What do you remember?"

I knew as soon as the words left my lips that asking had been a bad idea. Felicity wavered, then disappeared entirely, leaving me to clean up the mess she had made. Wasn't that the story of my life these days?

CHAPTER FOURTEEN

"Martha Tipton, you're a half-witted fool." Hands fisted on her hips, Bess Tate wrinkled her nose and glared. "Nobody wants to go on a picnic in Maine in the middle of February. Ain't nothing romantic about runny noses and frozen backsides."

Privately, I agreed with Bess.

"People sleep on blocks of ice in those ice hotels." Whenever anyone disagreed with her, Martha turned mutinous. "And they pay big money to do it, too."

In another minute, she'd probably suggest we build one of those in the middle of town to attract tourists. And then Bess's head would explode.

"Ladies," I cut in since none of the others in the small group of women who planned town events seemed inclined to do anything about the bickering. "I'm sure, with all the fine minds in this room, we can come up with a workable solution."

Before my divorce, I'd done all the event planning

for the charity arm of my ex-husband's family business. Once Martha got a taste of my skills in that area, she'd drafted me to help with her quest to rebuild tourism in the town of Mooselick River.

The latest scheme, I'd come to suspect, was more for my benefit than that of padding the town coffers. Martha aimed to get me paired up with a man. Martha was going to be sorely disappointed.

I mean, she was nice enough and everything, so were the rest of the older women who worked tirelessly for the town, but I wasn't going to date some guy just because they thought I should.

"Bess is right." Siding with the most vocally contentious of the group might not win me any favors, but I had to call them like I saw them. "The average temperature in Maine in the middle of February is a little too cold for outdoor dining."

"What if we rented a couple dozen of those outdoor heaters?" Martha suggested. "They had them at the botanical gardens when they put on the Christmas light show."

"You mean that one you went to down on the coast last year?" Bess gave Martha a beady-eyed stare. "The one where you complained for a week how you should have worn Long Johns and a second pair of pants? Been a long time since I went on a date, but thermal undies ain't exactly my idea of romantic attire."

"What do you think, Everly?" Patricia Croft had no way of knowing how hard I'd been biting the inside of my cheek to keep my composure, and to stave off the visual of Bess on a date. Or in thermal underwear. Or in underwear period.

I needed more information. "How does this basket lunch auction thing work again?" Other than the occasional girl's night at Cappy's Tavern, where I watched the mating dance of the inevitably drunk, I had little sense of the singles scene in town.

"It's stupid." Bess put in her two cents worth. "And it's sexist." That was a word I hadn't expected to hear her say.

Sitting in her chair at the head of the table—we met in the back of the town office—Martha took offense. "What are you on about? There's nothing sexist about a basket lunch."

"You might as well just put every single woman in town in hooker clothes and auction them off to the highest bidder. It amounts to the same even if you're trying to romanticize it by calling it a picnic date."

Seated to my left, Patricia let out a tiny snort. I so wanted to do the same.

"That's a hideous thing to say." Outrage rang through Martha's voice. "You're a sour old thing with a shriveled-up prune for a soul."

"Well, it beats turning into a pimp." Bess leaned forward in her chair, pointing a gnarled and shaking finger at Martha. "What do you think of that?"

I felt Patricia's body shaking, and my mistake was turning my head just enough to see her face. Above tightly-pressed lips, her eyes twinkled with silent laughter. The kind of laughter that's contagious. My lips twitched, but I managed to maintain control.

"Why, I never!" Martha exclaimed.

Bess never missed a beat. "And that's half your problem right there."

"Okay. That's enough." If I didn't put a stop to this conversation soon, I'd be joining Patricia in a fit of the giggles.

"Excuse me for thinking we could top off the playground fund and make some romance at the same time." Arms folded, Martha glared at Bess.

Bess glared back. "Butt out of people's love lives, and keep your fingers out of town folk's pockets during heating season. Oil costs the earth these days, and we're all going broke just trying to stay warm."

"It's five hundred dollars, not five thousand. We'd only need fifty singles to pay ten bucks each. I doubt that's enough to break the bank," Martha pointed out with fake sweetness.

"Fifty single people?" Bess rolled her eyes. "In Mooselick River?"

"I think we can all agree the basket lunch is off the table." I made a poor choice of words.

"We need to do something to pull in that last five hundred dollars if we're going to have the play-ground updated by May." Martha glared at Bess, but she was talking to me. "If you have a better sugges-tion, I'd like to hear it."

Patricia was the one laughing, but somehow, I was the one getting the ice treatment from Martha.

"It's winter, we've had a lot of snow, and that means one thing in Maine. Snowmobiles."

Ice fishing and trail riding were some of the big tourist draws this time of year.

"The trails run right along the edge of town on the way to Hackinaw, so why not partner up with the snowmobile club and see if we can come up with something fun? Maybe do our take on a poker run."

Arms still crossed over her ample bosom, Martha maintained her stoic expression. She might be using the argument with Bess as fuel, but when she asked how I planned to turn a poker run into a romantic Valentine's day venture, it seemed she was still set on the idea of finding me a man. Even if her intentions were good, and that was a given, I didn't appreciate the meddling.

Finally in control of herself, Patricia spoke up. "You can't count on having enough snow for trail-riding in mid-February—even if we have plenty on the ground now. One good thaw would send the whole thing down the tubes, and for what? We have months yet to come up with the rest of the playground money."

Tapping her fingers on the table, Martha had to admit, "You're right, Patty."

I sensed a *but* coming.

"But—" And there it was. "We have to do something, don't we? Look how much attention we got for the lighting contest."

Well, duh, there was a murder at the lighting contest, and a high profile one at that.

"Listen." I decided to toss an idea out there. "There are plenty of people who are single by choice, and even more who would be mortified to participate in a public dating ritual. Why don't we dispense with trying to pair people up and focus on helping people feel less lonely on Valentine's Day."

I had their attention.

"You've got that look on your face." Martha lit up. "You have an idea."

"I do. I think we should sponsor an event to bring awareness to shelter animals. Specifically to get as many of them adopted as we can. We'll host it here in town, advertise the event state-wide, and raise the playground money by selling something during the event. I'm thinking homemade dog treats, maybe."

"I don't hate it," Martha mused. "And getting animals out of shelters is a noble cause."

Bess was a cat person, and Patty raised chinchillas, so they were all in for anything that helped animals. With Martha on board, we hit the planning stage with a vengeance, and I added calling shelters to see how many would participate to my list of things to do for the week.

Best of all, I'd put an end to Martha's matchmaking efforts, at least for the time being. I felt good about the plan when I left the town office and headed toward Curated Collections.

"What are you doing?"

I wasn't actually trying to sneak up on Jacy and Neena when I slipped through the back door of the shop, but because they were standing side by side with binoculars practically pressed up against the front windows, neither woman heard me come in.

"You shouldn't scare a pregnant woman like that," Jacy had one hand pressed to her belly, the other to her heart. She searched my face for signs of distress but didn't bring up the topic of Winston, for which I was thankful.

"Sorry, I thought you heard me come in." Leaning first right and then left, I tried to get a look out the window, but Jacy was in the way, so I moved over closer to Neena. "What's going on? Fender bender?"

Neena reluctantly handed me her binoculars and stepped back to let me take her place. "Not exactly. We've been enjoyin' the show at the place next to the bait shop."

With the cold snap digging its claws into the January day, we were right in the middle of bundle-up season, but a good look at the back of the man painting the wall opposite the window could heat a woman's blood better than any warm coat.

"Still no idea what's going in there?" There was no sign on the building yet, so it was anyone's guess.

"Oh," Jacy said, reaching around to press her fist against her lower back, then waddled over to settle on a love seat that was for sale. "We have no idea. I've been trying to get Neena to run over and check things out, but she refuses to go. As if I can't be left alone for five minutes. Peanut isn't due for almost a month."

Neena turned and fisted her hands on her hips. "I would if I could trust you to stay out of trouble for that long."

As close as the two women had become during the process of opening a business together, they still bickered like children. Jacy rolled her eyes. "I'd have got myself out in another minute."

Neena tilted her head and explained. "This one was hankerin' for cucumbers yesterday, so I figured I'd be nice and go to the grocery store for some. I wasn't gone ten minutes, and what do I find when I come back?"

"Don't make it more dramatic than it was." Jacy took over and tried to downplay the story. "I went out back to grab a small bin of books because I wanted to put some on that nice shelf we took in the other day. But the bin was lighter than I expected, and I overbalanced when I stood up."

Shaking her head, Neena cut back in. "Overbalanced herself into a big box of throw pillows, is what she did. I came back from the store and found her wavin' her arms and legs around and lookin' like a flipped-over turtle."

"On a normal day, a customer would have helped me up, and you'd never have known anything happened," Jacy sulked.

Business had been slow everywhere in town since the start of the flu epidemic right before Christmas.

"Are you guys going to be okay if things don't pick up soon?" I gave Jacy a reprieve by changing the subject slightly. Businesses came and went pretty quickly in small towns. I'd hate for Curated Collections to be one of the ones that didn't make it beyond a few months.

Nodding, Jacy smiled at Neena. "We will because caution is Neena's middle name."

"Well, that makes me sound like an old maid, but when things were booming in the fall, I made sure we put back enough to cover us for a couple of months in case the late winter months were slow."

"We get a fair amount of local business when

people are out and about, more than enough to keep the doors open, and we've been expanding our online presence. But banking up some extra was a saving grace since we're not seeing more than the occasional tourist passing through."

"Don't say that in front of Martha," I said, shaking my head. "She's half ready to start a petition to build an ice hotel or something worse. I've only just stopped her from trying to turn the town into some sort of singles attraction for Valentine's day."

"That doesn't sound like the worst idea." Jacy had the same rabid light in her eyes I'd seen in Martha's, and I vowed then and there to keep those two away from each other at all costs. Neena would help, I could tell because she'd gone pale with horror.

Giggling, Jacy shifted into a more comfortable position on the love seat. "You should see your faces, the both of you. You look like deer in headlights."

Concentrating, I relaxed my face.

"I wasn't talking," she continued, "about the singles thing. Not specifically, but the ice hotel. There's something there."

Neena pressed her palm to her temple as if to stave off a sudden pain. "You can't be serious. Do you have any idea how much that would cost?"

"Not a hotel," Jacy flapped her hand to wave the notion away. "But what about doing something simpler, like an ice bar? I mean, I know you're trying to raise funds for the playground and all, but something that drew more traffic into Mooselick would benefit all the businesses in town."

I had to admit, the idea had merit, only with one or two drawbacks.

"A bar is good, but I'm not seeing much benefit to businesses that don't stay open late."

"That's easy," Jacy had a ready answer. "We could do two versions, one that's open earlier for the kids... maybe an ice cream bar with a Valentine's theme. Then, in the evening, change over to an adult venue."

"Get Cappy's to supply and sell the liquor, and the Kiwanis club to handle the ice cream, then we could sell raffle tickets to benefit the playground fund." Neena got into the swing of it. "Of course, the cost of the ice blocks and someone to carve them is the only wild card, but I'm betting you know someone for that, right Everly?"

"I might." One name popped into my head. "Let me make a call before I talk to Martha. This might be a better idea than the one I had for doing a pet adoption event because more businesses stand to benefit.

Though it does have the potential for her to twist it into some type of romantic thing."

"Maybe there's a way to do both. Either way, I'm sure you can rein her in, and now that I've solved your Martha problem, you owe me." Jacy's wicked grin sent my good spirits into a nosedive. "I promise not to move from this spot unless a customer shows up so you can go over and see what's what at the new place. The curiosity isn't good for Peanut."

"You know," Neena said, turning to me, "she's going to give Peanut a complex if she keeps using that baby as an excuse to get her own way."

Jacy threw Neena a saucy grin. "Peanut will not be denied. Now, go and bring me back news. I'm languishing for the lack of scandal."

"How did we get from *there's a new business in town, and we should check it out* to *scandal?*"

"Did you see the muscles on that guy? A man that fine just automatically comes with scandal."

CHAPTER FIFTEEN

"I can't believe she talked us into this." Neena kept her head carefully turned away from the shop window where Jacy was, without a doubt, peering at us through binoculars to keep from missing anything.

"Most of Jacy's ideas should come with a kicky little soundtrack playing in the background. The kind that indicates shenanigans are afoot. If I had a nickel for every time she talked me into doing something questionable … well, I'd have many dollars in my pocket, but I'd have missed out on some youthful indiscretions that were fun at the time."

"I'll want to hear more about that later." Reluctantly, Neena pulled open the door and pitched her voice loud enough to be heard. "Hello! It's just your friendly neighbors from across the street."

Without waiting for an invitation, I followed her into the over-heated room filled with the scent of fresh paint.

The half-naked man and new business owner, presumably, stood on a plank that spanned the distance between two metal stepladders and was in the middle of masking off the upper molding.

"Hey, save me a trip, and pass me a fresh roll of painter's tape." There was humor and warmth in the baritone of his voice as it drifted over his shoulder. "In the bag on the floor by the door."

Since I was closest, I did the honors.

"Here." I stepped nearer the ladder and held the tape up to him. He still hadn't introduced himself, though neither had we, and from below, I couldn't get a good look at his face.

"Thanks. Much appreciated."

Moving back to stand with Neena, I watched the play of muscles across his back while he tossed the empty roll across the room into the trash can. Scored himself a nice two-pointer, then finished applying the last two feet of tape.

"Perfect. Now," the man said, turning to us, "did you say you were neighbors?" He grabbed the tee shirt hanging on the top rung of one of the stepladders, shrugged it on, then lightly jumped the three feet down to the floor.

Unable to help myself, I studied his face because

it seemed so familiar to me, though I didn't think we'd ever met. I'd have remembered eyes that blue, and the feeling of safety that washed over me when he smiled.

"I'm Neena Montayne, I own Curated Collections—or half of it anyway." She waved a hand in the direction of the shop and then waited for his response.

"Drew," He poked a thumb toward his chest. "Andrew Parker."

"Nice to meet you." Neena shook hands with him, leaving me with no other option but to do the same.

So many experiences bring with them a sense of anticipation, the weightless moment on a high dive just before you slice into the water, or when your horse gathers her muscles to gallop. Or when a certain man holds out his hand for yours.

I didn't want to feel this way. Not now—not ever, and certainly not about a virtual stranger. I didn't believe in love at first sight. I still don't, but I couldn't deny that something sprang up between us, probably lust if I really wanted to put a name to it.

"Everly Dupree." My face felt hot as I struggled to drag my name up from memory.

"It is a pleasure." His voice was a warm blanket on a cold night.

"Yes, well." I pulled my hand from his and cleared my throat, which had gone dry as dust. "We came by to welcome you to town."

"And, to be nosy. If you don't mind me askin', what's this going to be when you're finished?" Neena's voice echoed off the bare walls.

Drew turned his attention to her, but reluctantly. "I'm opening a gym." With a body like that, what else could it have been? "Or I guess you could call it more of a fitness center. My cousin Riley's going in on it with me. She'll offer yoga sessions. The hot kind, as you can probably tell by the temperature in here. I'm testing the heating system."

"I've heard of that," Neena said. "It's basically doing yoga in a sauna, right?"

"Close enough." He grinned. "And during the day when we're keeping the place at normal temperatures, I'll be offering classes in self-defense and martial arts." He pointed toward the offset hallway leading to more space in the back. "We'll have fitness machines in the empty room to the left, lockers are already installed on the right. And that's basically the grand tour." His smile included both of us. "I've got a schedule in the back. Let me get one for you."

As soon as he was out of sight, Neena waggled her eyebrows at me and nodded.

I shook my head. She smirked and nodded again.

It was the wordless equivalent of her singing the *Everly and Drew sitting in a tree K-I-S-S-I-N-G* song with me uttering a silent protest. It lasted until we heard him coming back.

"Here." He handed us each a sheet of paper with a neatly-typed list of classes. "There's something for everyone. Don't tell Riley I said so, but her yoga classes for couples are going to be a big hit."

Neena must have sensed the subtle question because she answered for both of us. "That's one we'll have to miss since neither one of us is part of a couple right now."

Thank you for providing too much information.

"Then you really should take my self-defense class. Just the thing for single women."

Before Neena could confirm our intention to attend, I dragged her out of there and back to the shop where Jacy was not sitting on the love seat as promised but had been watching the show with her binoculars.

"Get in here and tell me everything. I suck at reading lips," she said.

Neena took off her coat and served herself a cup of coffee from the pot she kept going in case customers wanted some. "His name is Andrew Parker. He's opening a gym with his cousin Riley, and if I read the signs right, he'd like to engage in a little hand-to-hand training in the hope it leads to a lot of body-to-body contact with Everly."

My face flushed hot. "He does not."

"Oh, I think he does. There was a definite vibe."

"Andrew Parker." Jacy frowned and repeated his name a couple of times. "Sounds familiar."

"He goes by Drew if that makes a difference," I said.

Apparently, it did. Jacy snapped her fingers. "Drew Parker." Then she frowned again, and, grabbing the binoculars, took another look across the street. "Turn around so I can see your face," she muttered.

"You know he can't hear you, right?"

Jacy shushed me and kept watching. "Hah," she finally put the binoculars down. "I do know him. You should, too, since he spent a couple of weeks up at the lake one summer and hung out at our camp with my brother the entire time."

"I thought he looked familiar, but I don't remember ever meeting him. Are you sure we were there at the same time?"

Neena pointed her coffee cup toward Jacy. "She gets salty if you question her memory," she warned.

"And still, you do it." Jacy wrinkled her nose. "It would have been ..."—she stared at the ceiling while she tried to remember— "Fourth grade. The first week in July. I remember because my uncle tossed a handful of firecrackers in the campfire, and my mother said a word you never hear her say. Daddy told her not to cuss in front of Drew, and Drew said his father used that word a lot."

None of it rang a bell with me. "I wouldn't have been there, anyway. We always spent Independence Day with Grammie Dupree. Well, except for the year we went to Vermont. I think I was in—"

"Fourth grade," Jacy said it with me. "That explains it."

"I suppose we might have crossed paths for an hour or two, but I truly can't remember."

"So the man has family ties to town, then? That explains why he decided to open up shop here. Who else is he related to? The name Riley doesn't ring a bell."

That was where Jacy's memory went hazy. "I'll call Momma Wade later. She'll know. But I bet there's a story there. No one ups and moves to Mooselick River on a whim. We're not that kind of town."

I didn't bother to point out the number of transplants we'd had over the years—Neena included. At least the speculation about Drew's origins had taken the focus off his response to me, and I wanted to keep it that way.

Finally, with the salacious, man-ogling part of the day behind us, Jacy asked about Winston, and I had to tell the whole story of finding his body.

"At the risk of sounding like a horrible person, I'll be honest and say I'm not sure how I feel about his death. I liked him well enough the few times we met while I was married to Paul, but he wasn't a huge fixture in our lives." Saying so sparked the memory of Reva touting Winston as one of Paul's closest friends. Things must have changed since our divorce. "I've had it in my head Winston was a horrible person because of the way he treated me the day everything blew up. Looking back, I might have been transferring some of my anger with Paul to him."

"Well, he must have done something to somebody to get himself killed like that." As always, Jacy cut right through to the heart of things.

Still, I knew I'd turned some kind of corner, and if there was a way to help find Winston's killer, I'd give it a shot. Even big fat jerks deserved justice.

That thought followed me home.

CHAPTER SIXTEEN

"Get that tennis ball." I stood on the back porch, my laughter forming frosty plumes while Molly hopped, pounced, and stuck her head down into the snow. "You silly thing, you're just pushing it deeper into the snow."

Molly didn't care, and I didn't even mind the cold since she needed the romp almost as much as I needed to laugh. We were five days into the new year, and my hopes for making a fresh start hinged on putting an end to the final chapter of my old one. That probably meant helping Winston, but I hadn't the first clue where to start.

And he wouldn't be any help even if he ever showed up again.

With no plan in my head, I played with Molly until she tired herself out and went back inside to reheat a bowl of stew for lunch. I'd just put my dishes into the dishwasher when I got a call from a barely coherent Alicia.

"It's dad. He's—"

It sounded bad, and I didn't hesitate. "Just hang on, I'm on my way."

I found Alicia standing in front of the vending machines in an alcove down the hall from her father's room.

"I'm so glad you came." Alicia introduced me to her aunt, a rangy woman named Denise with the same kind smile and warm brown eyes as her brother.

"It's good to meet you, though I wish it were under better circumstances," I said, and let my gaze travel past the two women toward room number 315. "Is it good or bad news?"

With shaking fingers, Alicia stabbed the buttons for her choice of snack.

"Three doctors are in with him now, but we're not allowed to know what's happening."

"Is he—?" My face must have spoken for me because Alicia shook her head.

"No. It's not bad news. I don't think."

"He's awake," Denise explained. "They're testing his cognitive functions to determine the extent of possible recovery. That's how they termed it. Possible recovery."

I didn't know what else to say, so I settled in to stay and wait with them. "What can I do to help?"

"Just stay." Alicia grabbed my hand, and I pressed my warm fingers against her chilled ones while she told me the police might have new information about his attacker.

Maybe Denise was always quiet, or it was just the tension, but while Alicia chattered, she said little.

"There's a police officer named Jody Basset who checks in every few days. She's really nice. Our neighbors and some other friends came together to put up some money so we could offer a reward for any information that leads to an arrest. Now that he's awake, finding who hurt him matters more, you know?"

"Why didn't you tell me? I'd have pitched in."

"I didn't even know until it was already done, but it worked. Someone came forward with a video taken about a half a block away at the time when the police think the attack occurred. There's a guy running from the right direction, and because of the timing, Officer Basset says they're calling it a credible lead."

"That's great news."

"It is." Denise took a sip of vending machine coffee, wrinkled her nose at the cup, and got up to toss it in the trash. "The images were blurred, but they got enough to post a photo on all the news sites and ask for information that would help determine the identity of the possible assailant. It's just a matter of time before they can bring him in for questioning, we hope." Her eyes flicked toward Albert's room every few seconds.

"The guy they're looking for is a white male, between twenty-five and thirty, between five-nine and six feet tall, blue eyes and short blond hair," Alicia recited as though she'd memorized the list.

Just based on her description, the man who'd attacked Albert sounded a lot like my ex-husband.

"I hope they catch the guy, but right now, I just hope the doctors come out soon."

Thankfully, the wait was a short one, and after stopping just outside Albert's door for a brief conversation with his colleagues, Dr. Maron joined us.

"We've notified the police," he told Alicia. "As requested, once he regained consciousness. They've requested no visitors until they've had a chance to speak to him."

"Good. Fine." She flapped an impatient hand. "Move on to the important stuff. How is he?"

Nobody gives a good blank face like a doctor.

"He has some short-term memory loss, and he's

not fully oriented to time and place. You need to be prepared for the process to take some time, but for now, I'm encouraged by what I've seen. Given the severity of the head injury, he's doing far better than I'd expected."

"Does he remember me?" Clenched in her lap, Alicia's fist bore the white-knuckled evidence of her fear. "Will he recognize me when I see him?" Denise slid over and wrapped an arm around her niece for support.

"He was asking for you."

Her throat worked, and she only nodded.

"You'll need to wait just a bit longer, I'm afraid. As I said, the police want to speak to him first, and I've agreed, but only under my supervision. After that, you're free to go back in. Try not to tire him out, and don't push his memory too hard. Let things happen gradually."

With that, Dr. Maron put a hand on Alicia's shoulder and gave it a squeeze.

Joy suffused her face with a smile through tears. "Okay." She wobbled over to the chairs and sat down. "Okay," Alicia repeated. "I can breathe again."

"I'll just come back another time." I hugged Alicia and Denise as well before I left them. For once, the hospital smells didn't bring a sense of foreboding, but meeting the detective from Winston's death and Officer Bassett coming the other direction did. I nodded and hoped to slide right past them, but it was not to be.

"Ms. Dupree. If I could have a word," said detective Whatshisname, who wore no name tag or visible badge to offer a useful reminder.

"Sure." I let him direct me toward a bench near the window at the end of the hall where patients could sit and look out at a beautiful view of the river. "What can I do for you?"

"You can give us your whereabouts between nine p.m. and midnight on the thirty-first of December."

"Easy, I was here from seven or so until a little after eight. Then I went home and played board games with several of my closest friends. My attorney, Patrea Heard, was with me the entire time."

That widened the detective's eyes slightly.

"You were here on the night in question? May I ask why?"

Jacy would kill me if I mentioned her unfortunate intestinal issue. "One of my guests for the evening experienced a minor medical emergency. While I was here, I ran into Alicia Runyon, and since she was here alone, and scared, and I'd worked with her father, she asked me to stay. Her father had begun to show signs of regaining consciousness, and she needed someone with her while the staff assessed his condition. You can ask Dr. Maron if you like. He saw me here."

The detective said he would do just that, and then handed me copies of the video stills of the suspect in Albert's attack.

"Do you recognize this man?" Jody Bassett watched me with hawk-like attention as I leafed through the images. "Is it Paul Hastings?"

Did I want it to be him? Maybe a little, but not enough to lie or even to let my imagination run riot over my common sense. So I went through the series of images once, twice, three times to make sure.

Dressed in dark, shapeless clothing, a ball cap pulled low enough to cover all but the curve of one cheek and the suggestion of the shape of the chin, I couldn't be sure if I was looking at Paul or not.

"Alicia says you're looking for a man with light hair and blue eyes. I can't see his hair or his eyes in these." I picked one of the photos out from the group and looked at it more closely. Even slanted it so more light from the windows fell over it.

"Are you saying you can't identify this man from

these images?" Bassett and the detective exchanged a look. I knew what it meant.

"Hey, I like Albert much better than my ex-husband, so if I could say for sure this was Paul, I would do it in a heartbeat. I'm not interested in protecting him. Not at all. Not after everything he's done to me. I'd tap dance in the middle of the street if he got some of what's coming to him, but I also don't hate him enough to say this is him if it isn't."

Basset looked convinced, the detective not so much.

"Please look one more time, Mrs. Hastings."

"Dupree," I corrected. "My last name is Dupree."

Slowly, I went through the images again. "The build is close, but it's hard to tell for sure. I can tell you that Paul never owned anything that fit like that while I was married to him. He was far too vain to let inferior fabrics touch his precious skin." That sounded a bit more venomous than I intended.

"These were taken after the attack?"

Bassett nodded.

"The posture's wrong, but maybe that could be accounted for by assuming he panicked. And this here," I pointed, "looks like a shadow below the chin, but I can't tell for sure. If it is, then the shape's off, too. Paul's chin is squared off, this one looks more rounded. Honestly, I can't say with any degree of certainty that this is Paul Hastings. I'm sorry."

The detective might have pushed me more, but Bassett urged him to let it go, so he only asked. "Would you be willing to come down to the station and look at the raw footage?"

"Today?"

"We could send it to you if you'd rather, and then you could call me with your impressions." Bassett handed me two cards with her name, badge number, and contact information on them.

"Of course." I wrote down my email on one of them and gave it back to her. "I hope Albert remembers something that will help. He's a good man."

With that, I let them get on with talking to him and hoped they wouldn't take too long. Alicia needed to see her father.

CHAPTER SEVENTEEN

Since I was in town anyway, I offered to take Patrea to lunch.

"I thought I'd have information to report, but I can't get anything out of him." Patrea speared a meatball and wrapped spaghetti around her fork. We'd toasted—with our lemon water since it was the middle of a workday—to Albert's progress and moved on to a new topic. "The guy's mouth is sealed up tighter than Fort Knox, but he knows something even if he doesn't know he knows."

"Offering Winston's paralegal a job was a stroke of genius," I said. "But I feel bad that you're paying out more money on my behalf. I have a decent job, I can easily get a mortgage on the house to cover his salary."

Patrea laughed and dabbed sauce off her chin. "I didn't do it for you. Hiring William Deal was good business for several reasons."

"How so?"

"I've signed on enough of Winston's former clients to cover Bill's salary at least twice over, and I'm sure I'll pick up a few more because they like seeing a familiar face in the office. Using him to investigate Winston's death is a bonus. Or it would be if I could get him to unclench a little."

Like I said, genius.

Lucio had a way with carbonara, and I didn't regret letting Patrea pick the spot for our lunch date. "I can see why he'd be hesitant to dish dirt on his former employer to his new boss. If he talks, he proves himself disloyal, which isn't something most people want in an employee."

"True," Patrea considered. "I was surprised he accepted my offer. I've never made any bones about my disdain for Winston Durham. Not to speak ill of the dead, but he was a—to use your favorite term—sleaze-weasel."

"There you go. We need a different approach." I tugged my phone out of my purse and found nothing in my inbox from Officer Basset. "Not that I have the foggiest idea what it should be."

"I do, but you're not going to like it."

"I've been told not to leave the area." After turning up the volume on the alert tones, I dropped my phone back into my purse. "Which means I'm still a suspect even though I have an ironclad alibi. Short of delivering your newest employee a strip-o-gram, I'll probably be on board with whatever you think will work."

A less than delicate snort made me whirl to see Amber hovering behind me.

"Miss Prude," she said, pointing at me, "delivering a strip-o-gram. That'd be the day."

Since I couldn't tell her to shut up, I offered a rude hand gesture under the table and out of Patrea's line of sight.

"You're on the right track, but a stop farther down the line than I was thinking. Bill's single. Painfully so, I'd say. I was thinking that arranging for him to go on a date might be in order."

"I haven't been on a date since Paul, but I suppose I could—"

"Not with you."

I took offense and then wondered why, since I didn't want to go on a date with Bill anyway. "You don't think I'm his type? Or that I couldn't vamp some answers out of him? I assure you, I can be quite charming when I put my mind to it. Sexy, too."

Patrea wisely kept her expression in check when

she saw my flaming face. Red hair and pale skin made me a natural blusher.

"I have no doubt." Even so, I heard the humor in her voice and started to call her on it, then decided not to humiliate myself by defending my sexiness. "But that wasn't what I meant. He knows who you are."

"Oh." I caught on. "Then, who?"

"Maybe we could ask Neena."

We talked for a few more minutes about how we could set it up if Neena agreed. And that was a big if. I knew she wasn't ready to date, not that this would be an actual date, but even so, we'd had that conversation more than once.

Remembering Amber, I turned, but she'd taken herself off to wherever it was she went when she wasn't haunting me. Probably somewhere she could laugh at me in peace.

"Speaking of dating, how are things with Chris? Or did he decide you weren't worth an hour of winter driving?" I knew the answer already. Chris was no sleaze-weasel.

"He's commuting at the moment. I had to clear out dresser and closet space for him. It's weird how well he fits right in, but do you want to know what's weirder? I miss the farm."

Neat and orderly, Patrea's townhouse was the polar opposite of the old farmhouse Chris had taken over from his parents when his dad retired from Christmas tree farming.

"It's not weird at all. Underneath all that plaid flannel, Chris has a touch of the urbanite in him, and under your spit-and-polished power-suit exterior lurks the heart of a country girl. You just needed to unbend a little."

Patrea checked to make sure no one was listening. "That man has enough moves to unbend a pretzel."

I was trying to come up with a suitable response when my phone made the plink-plink sound of my email alert.

"It's the video from Albert's attack." I'd told her about the reward and the new evidence. "I'm nervous to look at it. What if it is Paul, and he attacked Albert because of whatever was in that envelope he gave me?"

"If it is, you have to know it's not your fault."

Easy to say, not as easy to believe after spending time with Alicia. But I had to know, so I tapped play while Patrea got up to look over my shoulder.

"Is it Paul?" She asked after I'd run the video twice.

"It's hard to tell on a screen this small." The detective wasn't going to be happy with me.

At Patrea's request, I forwarded her a copy of the video before I headed home to Mooselick River to talk Neena into going on a date.

"Molly, my girl, it looks like I'll need to break out a bribe." So saying, I grabbed the key from the hall table and unlocked the door to the addition. "I think I remember reading something in Catherine's diaries about a set of high-quality sable brushes she'd stashed away, unused, in a drawer."

"That's sad, don't you think?" Amber had returned. "Saving things for a later that never comes." The thought apparently bummed her out, because she faded away again, leaving me to wonder what she regretted not doing in her life. Probably plenty of things since she'd died so young.

Contemplating the difference between regretting the things you didn't do and the things you did, and considering that regrettable acts were probably why Winston was dead, I hunted through the drawers in Catherine's studio for the brushes. I intended to give them to Neena even if she decided she didn't want to help. It was right that they go to someone who would put them to good use.

"I can't take those." An hour later, Neena looked at me in horror. "Do you know how much they're worth?" She named a figure in the hundreds of dollars and then said with emphasis, "Each."

"Okay," I said. "But you'd use them, right? I mean, if you had a set of these, you'd paint with them."

"Of course, I'd use them. They were made to be used."

"Then, you'll use them, and you'll paint amazing things, and they'll fulfill their destiny." Finally, I got to the point of my visit. "I have a favor to ask, and you shouldn't consider the brushes to be a bribe."

I told her about Patrea's idea and asked for her help. "What do you say? It wouldn't be a date, it would be a spy mission."

A slow smile spread over Neena's face. "Like Mata Hari?"

"Minus the circus act, exotic dancing, and seduction, but sure."

"So all of the spying, none of the fun?"

She was in, I could tell. "You get him to answer a few questions, and you can do whatever you want with him. Can I tell Patrea to set it up?"

"Can I borrow one of those fabulous dresses languishing the shadowy depths of your closet?"

"My closet is your closet." I sent Patrea the text. She responded immediately to say she'd get back to me with a place and time. "The wheels are in motion, but no pressure, okay? You can back out at any time."

"The guy's not a murder suspect." Neena looked to me for confirmation, and I shook my head. "So the worst that can happen is I go on a tedious date and don't get any useful information." She held out her hands as if using them to weigh options. "But I'll be wearing that hot little blue designer number of yours. The one with the scooped back and the beading over the bodice."

She could keep the dress if she pulled this off. We made a short list of the information that would be most helpful to get from Bill Deal before I walked home in the dark.

"I owe you an apology." Winston fell into step beside me in the middle of the street.

"Only one?" I could have cut him some slack considering the look of misery on his face, but he'd picked the exact wrong time to pop up. Even if Neena regarded her upcoming date as something exciting and fun, I blamed Winston for putting her in the position of having to help him. No one deserved to be murdered, and I still felt sympathy for him in death, but everyone from my former life was turning out to be a pain in the tail.

"Count again. And do it from somewhere else. I'll help you get into the light, but I'm doing it for me, not you. If you really want to help, give me something to work with. Maybe it was you who forged my initials and signature on the prenup, or were you in cahoots with Paul over the mess at the foundation? Do you know who bashed Albert on the head? Did it have to do with me? Why don't you just admit to all of your crimes and tell me where to find proof."

If there's one thing I've learned, it's that asking a ghost for information surrounding their death is a surefire way to make them go poof for a while. When I verbally poked at him again, Winston vibrated so quickly he turned into a fading blur.

"Good riddance," I said to the spot where he'd been, but the argument had sparked an idea. What if Winston made a habit of forgery? Maybe Paul wasn't the only one he'd altered documents for, and perhaps he'd screwed over someone who cared about money more than I did.

Inside, I booted up my laptop and discovered the

only way to see divorce records from the vital statistics bureau was to search by the name of one of the parties. If I knew that, I wouldn't need a list, so I gritted my teeth and searched the newspaper's website for the term divorce. Mine, of course, popped up with some splashy speculative pieces, none of them casting me in the best light, but it wasn't the most recent divorce scandal. That honor went to Honor.

Honor St. Jacques to be more specific. She and her husband, Andre, had split after fifteen years, and according to the article, the rift had not been amicable. Winston wasn't mentioned, but I still felt the tingle and buzz in my blood. From what I read, Honor's situation and mine were quite similar.

—Andre St. Jacques. One of Winston's clients?

I sent a text message to Patrea. Fifteen minutes later, she called.

"He was, why?"

Citing the newspaper article and not my conversation with Winston, I outlined my suspicions that Winston had been the instigator behind the forgery of my prenuptial agreement instead of Paul.

"Could be, but even so, they were in it together."

"Oh, I know, but if he did it once, he might have

done it twice. Could be a motive for murder, so I did a little digging and came up with Honor St. Jacques."

"You think she killed him?"

I'd met Honor a few times at various functions and remembered her being the type of woman who drank a lot and laughed a little. Beyond that, I couldn't say.

"Maybe. I know her well enough to compliment her shade of lipstick but not to borrow it. Certainly not well enough to form a solid opinion of whether she's capable of murder. Still, I think I'd like to talk to her about her divorce. See if she's in the *Winston screwed me over* club."

Over the phone, I heard Patrea's fingers tapping on the table, a habit of hers when she was thinking through a problem.

When she spoke, she sounded doubtful. "I know she had money of her own before she hooked up with Andre. I can't remember if she had more or less than him, though."

"Begs the question of how much she has now, doesn't it? With me, it was a different setup altogether. I had nothing coming into the marriage and no expectations of leaving with anything if it didn't work out. I figured the forgery had to do with Paul setting me up to take the fall for misappropriation of funds, but maybe I was wrong, and it was Winston." For whatever reason, and that was the wild card.

"The Arts Council dinner is this week."

"I know," I said. "I got an invitation. Somebody must have missed the memo that I'm persona non grata with the society set." It had come to my current address, too. "Are you planning to attend?"

"I'm taking Chris."

"Okay, now I almost want to go, because that's going to set some tongues wagging, and I'd like to watch."

I heard the smile in her voice. "Half the reason I'm going. But you should come. Honor's more likely to talk to you since you're lipstick buddies and all."

Did I want to subject myself to that level of scrutiny? The buzz around me hadn't quite died down, and at least one of my former in-laws would probably attend.

"I'll think about it."

CHAPTER EIGHTEEN

"You"—I pointed my finger at Jacy—"are on my list."

"What did I do?"

My mock glare bounced off her like a rubber ball off a wall. "I'll tell you in a minute."

I waited for the customer she was ringing up to leave, and while that happened, I got myself a cup of coffee from the dispenser.

"Martha loves your ice bar idea."

"Hey! I helped. Score one for the peanut shell."

Frowning, I looked to Neena for an explanation. She raised an eyebrow but smiled when she explained. "Peanut." She pointed to Jacy's belly. "Peanut shell." She pointed to Jacy.

"Cute. I see what you did there. But this ice bar thing is not so cute. I just got a call from the ice sculptor to verify the changes Martha made to the order and to see if he could send me a new copy of the bill so I could authorize the added expenses."

"I don't see how whatever she's done is my fault." Not the least bit concerned, Jacy left her stool behind the counter in favor of the softer, more comfortable love seat that still hadn't sold. "But make me a cup of dandelion, would you? There's a box of biscotti over there somewhere, too."

"I live to serve. Anyway, Martha decided that we needed a statement piece—that's what the sculptor called it, and I could hear the air quotes over the phone—so she asked if he could carve us a statue of Cupid on a heart-shaped plinth."

Over the lip of her teacup, Jacy's eyes twinkled. "That doesn't sound so bad."

"Did I mention she wanted the plinth lit up with red lights?"

"Still nice."

"And the Cupid done in white ice, not clear."

"Ooh! Pretty."

I delivered the clincher. "Fifteen feet tall."

Jacy giggled.

"He offered me a discount on the cost. It would have been a bargain at three grand since he normally charges four."

"Who did she think was footin' the bill?" Neena

had come in through the back just in time to catch the gist of what happened.

"No idea. I'm considering just giving her the money for the playground fund. Five hundred is little enough to spend to put an end to the madness and take Martha's mind off sticking her nose in my love life."

Rant over, I washed out my coffee cup and got ready to leave.

"I'll pick you up at quarter to seven," Neena said as my hand landed on the door handle.

I turned back to look at her curiously. "What for? Your date with Bill isn't for two more days."

"We're going to that self-defense class at Drew's place. Remember, he invited us when we were over there the other day."

"I remember him mentioning it, I don't remember saying I'd go."

Neena grinned. "Sugar, if I'm goin', you're goin', and I'm goin'. Any woman who lives alone should know how to defend herself. What if Bill, the paralegal, gets ideas?"

That last was a subtle reminder that I owed her. "So I'll pick you up at quarter to seven, and you'd better be ready."

And since she was right, and since I did owe her, I was ready on time.

"You've probably seen plenty of movies where someone disarms an assailant who's carrying a gun, right?" Drew's cousin Riley lectured as we all sat cross-legged on our mats and listened. "How many times have you seen the hero or heroine grab the gun and pull? That's a good way to get yourself shot."

Tall, with broad shoulders and a curvy build, Riley still looked almost dainty compared to him when she used Drew to demonstrate.

"See how he's holding the gun with his finger on the trigger? If I pull it toward me like they do in the movies, his automatic response is to resist. His finger tightens, and as I pull on the gun, it almost forces him to pull the trigger. But, if I do this—" Palm up, she slammed the heel of her hand hard against the end of the barrel. The force of the blow shoved the fake pistol right out of Drew's hand.

"I eliminate that automatic reflex, and the unexpected direction of movement causes him to drop the weapon."

Directing us to partner up—naturally, I chose Neena—Riley had us all practice the maneuver a few times before Drew took over the class.

"Pretend the pad is your attacker." Drew fitted his arm through the straps of a rectangular pad. "This is his torso."

He lifted the pad, braced in front of his upper body.

"You're going to grab him by the shoulders and pull down while bringing your knee up to make contact with his midsection. The goal here is to take the wind out of him, so aim just below the ribcage with your knee and use the pulling motion to add momentum to the blow."

Turning sideways so we could see, he moved toward Riley, who demonstrated the proper technique several times. Each time she brought her knee up to make solid contact with the pad, Riley yelled, "No."

"Okay," She said when she was done. "Now, it's your turn. Line up, single file, and don't be gentle. The pad will take most of the force, and Drew's prepared, so you won't hurt him. Use those knees like you mean business, ladies."

"Don't forget to use your voice," Drew said. "Tell your attacker no, and make it loud. The noise serves more than one function. It can draw the attention of bystanders who might come to your aid, and it brings the element of surprise. Voicing your power also increases the ferocity of your counter-strike."

I ended up in the middle of the line, so I had time to watch the women who went ahead of me. Some twittered, some seemed too preoccupied with Drew's muscles to follow his directions.

When it was my turn, I didn't hold anything back. The pad was harder, firmer than I expected, but when my knee made contact, the word *no* came up from somewhere deep inside me.

I said no to every person who had ever hurt me in the past. I said no to Paul, and to Reva, and to the situations that had turned my gut into a pit of fear. I took back my power, and it felt good. It felt primal.

And I wanted to do it again.

So I went to the back of the line, took another turn.

Most of the time, we go through life doing what needs to be done, and if anyone asked, we'd be reasonably confident we were awake and aware. I realized I hadn't been. Not entirely. Not with the same level of connectedness I felt when the force of the blow sang from my knee to my thigh.

"Don't hold back," Drew said my third time

around. "Give me everything you've got. I can take it."

Seeing Paul's face instead of his, I switched legs once, twice, then again and again until my hair hung in sweaty strings, my face burned red, and my breath came in pants and gasps.

"One day, you'll tell me what's behind all the pent-up aggression."

I shook my head and went back to stand with Neena and wait for what came next.

Where had this been all my life?

We moved on to punching and kicking with Drew demonstrating some of the finer points of where and how to hit to cause the most pain. Disable and escape.

"Turn your fist over, and sweep down. Aim for the bridge of the nose. A hard hit to that spot can break the nose, but at the very least will make the eyes water. Despite what you've been told, a man can still fight after he's been kicked in the misters, but he won't be as efficient if his eyes are watering."

"But one of those is far more satisfyin' than the other." Neena offered, and everyone laughed.

"If you have an opening to do both, take it. Whatever it takes to get the job done." Drew grinned and then offered one final lesson.

"If you control the head, you control the rest of the body." He asked Riley to demonstrate his point, which she did by slinging an arm around his head, and with a swift downward, twisting motion, sending her cousin to the mat. The maneuver ended with her kneeling on Drew's head.

Someone behind me snickered, but I could see how everything I'd learned might have helped me the day Hudson's killer had attacked me in my own home. Or the day when another murderer had gone after Jacy.

"And that works even if you're smaller than the person attacking you? Can't they just reach back and grab you?"

"Not as easy as you'd think." Riley kept her knee firmly planted and leaned over to press Drew's arm to his side. "Try to keep enough weight on the head to inhibit movement, but also spare enough to hold his arms. This technique creates something of a stand-off situation, so it's best used to buy enough time for someone to come to your aid."

Singling me out of the group, she demonstrated

again, offered a few pointers in a low voice, and then told me to give it a try.

"Don't hold back," Drew repeated. Order or challenge didn't matter to me. I needed this more than I needed to breathe. "Because I won't."

He came at me then, and I moved in. Lifted up on the balls of my feet, judged the distance, and sprang forward to wrap my arms around his head. The momentum carried me forward, gave power to the twist of my body. I bore him to the mat, ended just as Riley had shown, with his head pinned under my knee and my throat sore from my victory cry.

Nothing had ever felt this good.

"Everly." Drew's voice broke through the rushing in my head. "You wanna let me up now?"

"Oh, sorry." I stood, and this time, I didn't go to the back of the line, but stood alone and waited until the class had ended. The last to go, Neena joined me as Riley declared the class to be over.

"Do you need to head right home?" I asked. "I need a minute."

Neena waggled her eyebrows and allowed she had plenty of time, so I should take all I needed.

"Sign me up." I approached Drew. "I need more."

Neena might have misunderstood my reasoning, Drew did not. "Tuesday night."

I nodded, and as I turned to leave, I heard him say, "Whatever you need."

CHAPTER NINETEEN

The dark wig made my scalp itch, but between it and Jacy's skillful makeup job, even my own mother would have a hard time picking me out of a crowd as I strolled into the restaurant where Patrea had arranged a blind date. Bill certainly wouldn't recognize me as the hostess seated me alone at the table for two next to the one reserved for him and Neena.

"Will anyone be joining you tonight?" she asked.

"No. I'm sorry, it's just me." Why I was apologizing, I'll never know. Once she was gone, I scooted my chair and place setting to a position close enough to eavesdrop.

On the table, my phone vibrated.

—*He's on his way.* I read the message from Patrea.

—*We're good to go*, I relayed to Neena and settled in to wait.

"Everly? That is you, isn't it?" Drew's voice gave

me the shivers every time I heard it. What were the odds he'd show up here and now?

Then again, if he'd spotted me through the disguise, Bill might. I'd just have to hold my menu over my face or something.

"I ... uh ... I do have a good reason for all of this." I indicated my face and hair. "But I don't have time to explain it now." Bill would walk through that door any minute, and after waiting just long enough to have him worried he'd been stood up, Neena would arrive. That part had been her idea. She said it would put him off his game.

"You're meeting someone on the sly." Drew tilted his head and squinted at me. "Bookie? No. That's not it. Torrid affair with a married man?"

The disgust on my face made him grin.

"I'm not meeting anyone, and you have to go." I leaned sideways to look past him but didn't see any sign yet of the paralegal.

"Stalking someone? Or ... this is even better ... you're in the CIA and on a mission. That's it, right? You have a secret life."

We could not be having this conversation when Bill walked in.

"Me? I'm an open book. No secret life here." Except for being a ghost magnet, but that was another discussion we weren't having now. Or ever.

I turned the tables on him. "And what are you doing here? We're not in Mooselick River anymore, so you're probably on a date. Don't you think she'll be annoyed if she sees you hanging around talking to me?" The thought of him on a date hurt a little.

Drew threw back his head and laughed. "No, I'm not on a date. I think we both know who I'm interested in seeing. I'm a one-woman guy." He circled the table, leaned down close enough his breath shivered across my cheek. "You look good, Everly Dupree. But don't wear the wig on our first real date, okay?"

All of a sudden, I couldn't breathe. Or think. Or remember why I was there.

That was the moment Bill chose to walk through the door.

"You have to go." I snapped back to the present, my eyes on the other man as the hostess greeted him and made ready to lead him to his table. "I promise I'll explain later."

Drew turned his head to follow my gaze, saw Bill, and quirked a brow. "He doesn't look like your type."

"I don't have a type, but he's not here for me." As Bill was seated at the next table, I hissed, "See? Now, go. Please."

Curiosity piqued, Drew shook his head and whispered in my ear before settling into the seat opposite me. "I think I'll stay, and we can pretend we're on a date. Call it a preview for the real thing."

I closed my eyes and took a couple of deep breaths to settle my nerves. It was too late to do anything about the situation, so I picked up my menu, scanned the options, and made my choice as Neena walked into the room.

She'd chosen well when given access to my closet, and filled out the little blue dress better than I ever had. Well enough to draw plenty of attention from the men in the restaurant.

Drew picked up on my interest and turned his head to look. His eyes flicked back toward me once, then he watched Neena's progress toward the next table. Whatever he might have said got cut off as our server arrived to take our order.

"I'll have the garlic chicken." I cocked a brow at Drew.

"Well played," he murmured and ordered the same.

At the next table, Neena and Bill made first contact.

"Bill Deal?" Neena all but purred.

Stuttering at the magnitude of his good fortune, Bill introduced himself and gallantly rose to help Neena push in her chair.

The music of the south more pronounced in her voice than usual, Neena started out with the getting-to-know-you version of small talk designed to charm Bill into talking mostly about himself.

"Go, Mata Hari," I whispered as she got him talking about his work.

"What are you—" Drew's question ended abruptly when I reached across the table and surreptitiously pinched the back of his hand. Somehow, my attempt to shut him up ended with my hand trapped in his, but at least he wasn't talking.

"Oh my stars," Neena laid it on a little thick. "Do you mean the Winston Durham that was murdered?"

I went still and waited for Bill to answer.

"The very same."

"You must have some idea who had a reason to kill that poor man. Being right on the spot, and all."

If she ever decided to stop painting and shop

keeping, Neena could have had a career on the stage. She hit all the right notes.

"There's not much I can say without breaking attorney/client privilege." But it sounded like he wanted to, and who could blame him? Here was this gorgeous creature hanging on his every word.

Come on, Neena. Push just a little.

I heard her suck in a breath, which, based on the way that dress fit her, probably did exciting things to the bodice. "Oh, Billy. I wasn't askin' for names or anything personal." She lowered her voice a little. "But it's just so ... excitin'"—she put a lot of sexual innuendo into that one word— "to be around someone connected to such a scandalous crime. Isn't there somethin' you can tell me?"

The server took that moment to show up at their table. Neena ordered raw oysters and then asked for chocolate sauce. "Can you be a love and put that sauce in a container to go?"

With my attention focused on Neena, I'd almost forgotten about Drew until he made a low, choking sound. If he blew this for us, I'd take the first opportunity to see how well he handled a knee to the solar plexus without three inches of padding to take the hit.

I pinched him again, this time using my nails for a little added emphasis, and he managed to get his face under control as our food arrived. Amid the flurry of activity in getting the plates settled and making sure we had everything we needed, I lost the thread of Neena and Bill's conversation.

When I tuned back in, he was telling her—a long ramble, but put in the vaguest of terms—about how the ex-wife of one of Winston's high-profile clients was under investigation, and would probably be indicted on charges of fraud and money laundering. I knew he meant me, and it sounded like he thought I was Winston's killer.

Then he clinched it. "Once a criminal, always a criminal."

My jaw clenched so hard my teeth clacked together.

"I think I heard about that on the news. Weren't the police looking at the husband, too?"

Easy, Neena. I thought when her tone went a little sharper than it should. Easy.

By now, Drew was paying as much attention as I was to the conversation at the next table, and I wondered what he knew or thought he knew about me. Enough, probably, to fill in that gap anyway.

When he put his fork down and reached over to squeeze my hand, it seemed like I'd been right.

"The husband was a high-profile client."

As if that was the only measure of a man.

"Not just on the legal side of things, either. Winston managed Mr. Has—the husband's personal portfolio. Or some of it, anyway."

Now that was something I hadn't known, and now that I did, I had questions.

So, apparently, did Neena.

"Oh, really? I didn't know attorneys did that type of thing. How does it work?" I could imagine Neena propping her elbows on the table and leaning forward to listen intently.

"It's not uncommon," Bill said, "for an attorney to also provide financial advisory services for either a flat rate or a percent or two of the managed funds. Such an arrangement can be quite lucrative for both parties."

"Or it could be a motive for murder." Neena must have read my mind. "People make mistakes, after all. What if Winston lost the husband's money?"

There was a pause while Bill pondered. "I suppose that's a possibility. I didn't work with Winston on the financial side of his practice."

And a second pause while their meal arrived.

"Everything looks so delicious," Neena gushed. "Now, what were we talking about before?"

"Murder," Bill promptly answered. "Don't you think we should change the subject to something more palatable?"

By the slurping sound, I assumed Neena had chosen an oyster. "Oh no, I'm utterly beguiled. The whole time you worked there, you were inches away from danger. It makes me shiver just thinking about it. Danger turns me on."

Okay, that one even dragged a smile across my face, and I planned to mercilessly taunt Neena over it later.

"Certainly not," Bill disagreed. "I don't mind saying—and I told the police the same thing—I think Winston was killed over a personal matter, not a professional one. He was a stickler in the office. He made it a point to adhere to the letter of the law."

Ignoring Bill's changing stance on my role as murderer, I rolled my eyes at Winston being a paragon of legal virtue, and Drew quirked a brow at me. "I'll tell you later," I mouthed because after sitting with me this long, he deserved to know what he'd stumbled into.

"When you say personal, do you mean romantic-type personal or the friends-and-family kind?"

"All this talk of murder seems inappropriate for a first date. Why don't you tell me something about you? I can tell you're not from around here. What brought you to the frozen north?"

"A man, darling. What else? But I will confess something." She paused to whet his appetite for the revelation. "I normally hate first dates, and blind dates are the worst of the worst, but you've been a breath of fresh air. I could sit and talk to you all night."

That was my signal. Keeping it sheltered from Bill's view, I tapped Neena's contact number on my cell phone.

On cue, I heard her ring tone, and then her cheerful tones assuring him she needed to take the call.

"Oh, no!" Neena said to no one at all. "Is she all right? Are you sure? No, it's fine. I'm leaving right now." A pause. "I'm sorry, but I have to cut the evening short. There's a minor emergency. One of the children."

"Children?"

"Yes, of course. Didn't Patrea tell you about the children?"

"She must not have thought to mention them. How many do you have?"

Without missing a beat, Neena said, "Oh, just the six right now."

"Six." His tone was flat.

"Two sets of triplets."

Bill made no effort to follow her out or ask for a second date. He paid the bill and left while I finally started to pick at the food on my plate.

"That was—" Drew started to say.

"Yes, it was. This chicken isn't half bad. Do you want to go to a black-tie function on Friday?" I could swing the arts dinner at a hundred dollars per plate using Catherine's egg money, and feel pretty good about it since I thought she'd approve.

"Would it be a date? Or another covert ops mission?"

"Yes." I looked at him over the rim of my glass as he tried to figure out which question I'd answered. "But I'll be going as myself this time."

He leaned back in his chair, rested one arm on the table, and looked—I swear—right into me. "And who are you now?"

"Telling you," I said, waving my fork at him, "wouldn't be nearly as much fun as letting you figure it out on your own, now, would it?" Not long after my return to Mooselick River, Jacy chided me for not being the audacious woman she remembered, but when Drew laughed, that woman wakened inside me.

"Black tie, huh? Okay, I'm in."

"It's a date." Did those words come out of my mouth? Yeah, they did. "So how much of this little caper did you figure out on your own?"

"Enough to know you're mixed up in murder."

I waited for him to try and talk me out of pursuing any course of action that he might consider dangerous. He had to give it a shot, right? Or else hand in his alpha male card.

"I have my reasons," I said.

"I gathered as much." Since I wasn't eating it, Drew took my dinner roll, used it to mop up the last of the garlic sauce on his plate. "Tell me the parts of the story that weren't media fodder."

Before I did, I took a moment to weigh my options. If my life was a movie of the week, then Drew would be the too-good-to-be-true guy who shows up and gains the heroine's trust only to betray her in the end.

Oh wait, I'd already married that guy. What were the odds there'd be two of them?

Could I trust this man, though?

He saw my struggle.

"I'm not him," he said quietly and took the wind right out of my sails.

"No," I replied, "I guess you're not."

CHAPTER TWENTY

I stripped off the wig, tossed it on the passenger's seat, and pulled my phone out of my purse. I'd left the ringer off while Drew and I had finished dinner, and I was a little bit surprised by the number of missed calls and messages. Most were from Jacy or Patrea, but it was the photo message from Alicia that held my attention.

In it, Albert was propped up in bed, smiling lopsidedly, and giving the thumbs up. Alicia had captioned it with a series of heart emojis.

Me: Is he cleared for visitors? I asked. The response came back in seconds.

Alicia: Anytime tomorrow afternoon.

Me: I'll see you then.

I smiled all the way home and kept smiling even when I had to squeeze my car in past Jacy's and Patrea's. I even smiled when Molly growled at the wig in my hand as if she thought it might come to life and mount an attack.

"Hush, you silly girl." I stashed the wig out of sight and followed the sound of voices to the kitchen.

"Neena gave us the Bill story, now it's your turn."

"I'm sure she covered everything." I pretended to misunderstand and then had to duck a barrage of popcorn.

"I had dinner with Drew. It's not that big a deal, certainly not popcorn-worthy."

"We'll be the judge of that." Jacy picked up her bowl. "In the living room, though. I need to prop up my feet."

We spent the rest of the evening hashing over whether it had been a good idea for me to tell Drew my sordid story and if we'd really learned anything useful from Bill. And eating popcorn, naturally.

On Saturday morning, I called David and asked him to handle tenant calls for the evening, then spent another hour searching for the missing envelope before heading to the hospital to visit Albert.

Alicia met me at the elevators, her eyes misty over a wide smile. "How's he doing?"

She all but fell into my arms. "Good. It's good."

All I could do was hold her and babble some soothing nonsense as the sobs wracked her body. I am, by the way, a sympathy crier. By the time she'd let it all out, we were both blubbering.

Once the spate passed, we sat on the bench at the end of the hall.

"I thought everything would be easier when he woke up, but it's so much harder. He's trying so hard, but he gets agitated and says things that aren't nice when he can't find the right words."

I took her hand, gave it a squeeze.

"Dr. Maron prepared me for what to expect, and if anything, Dad's doing better than we hoped." Alicia twisted the hem of her sweatshirt while she talked. "But I feel like I can't breathe. Like my insides are being yanked out and twisted into pretzels. My dad is my rock. He's the one who has been there when I needed love or comfort, and now he doesn't always remember my name."

The pain in her voice pierced right through me. So did her bravery. I put an arm around shoulders too slight for the burden they'd had to bear.

"I'm being stupid," she said. "Dr. Maron calls my dad the Miracle Man because he's improving so rapidly, and I'm stupid for feeling crushed that he didn't wake up and jump out of bed like nothing happened."

"Don't downplay your response. I think the emotional roller-coaster is probably natural, given the situation. Have you talked to your aunt? She seems like a supportive person."

"She totally is. She dropped everything to come here and be with me. I can't begin to repay her kindness, so I try not to be a burden. She wasn't here when he woke up because she sold her house in St. Louis. She says since her kids are grown and spread all over the country, they can visit her here just as well as there."

"That's wonderful news." And it meant Alicia wouldn't be alone no matter what happened with Albert.

"It is." Alicia smiled. "Thank you, Everly. This helped a lot. Once you've had your whole life ripped out from under you, it's harder to trust that good things can still happen."

No wonder she'd needed a good cry. "If you ever need to vent, or just to talk, you can call me. Night or day." I hugged her again.

"He's going to be fine. Dr. Maron says if he keeps improving at this rate, there's no reason he can't make a full recovery. I know he's going to be fine."

"He'll heal much faster when he knows you

believe in him. The Albert I know would move heaven and earth for you."

She looked lighter, closer to her age than she had when I'd arrived.

"Do you want to see him? He can have visitors as long as you only stay a few minutes and don't tire him out."

"Of course."

Alicia kept hold of my hand as we walked down the hall to his room. "He's getting transferred to a different floor tomorrow." She raised her voice as we walked closer to the bed. "Old lazybones here is going to the rehab wing to get his butt whipped back into shape. Hey dad, look who I found out in the hall."

"Hello, Albert."

"I remember you. Sweet Miss Everly." Speaking in partial sentences, Albert worked hard at getting the words out. "Always asked about my Alicia."

"She's a lovely girl, Albert, and you were right to be proud of her."

"Good girl. Going to college. Good school."

Lopsided as it might be, his smile made my heart sing. "She deserves it. Aced the SAT, didn't she?"

Albert's expression went from slightly dazed but cheerful to sharp and perfectly lucid. He had something to say if he could get his body to cooperate with his mind.

"775 reading, 782 math. Important. Don't forget." With what looked like an enormous effort, Albert lifted his head off the pillow, his eyes bored into mine. "775 reading, 782 math. Promise you'll remember."

Giving his hand a pat, I repeated, "775 reading, 782 math. I'll write it down, so I won't forget."

"No. Don't write. Just remember."

I could tell Alicia thought I should leave, and I totally agreed with her.

"Okay, I won't write it down. Now, you need to rest, so you can get well faster. I'll come back another time."

Alicia didn't leave her father to follow me out, so I filed away her SAT scores in the recesses of my mind, and spent the drive back to Mooselick River thinking about the fragility of life.

CHAPTER TWENTY-ONE

"You don't belong here. You never did." Winston's ghost echoed my own misgivings, and with Drew standing next to me, I couldn't argue the point. For the first few months of my marriage, attending these functions felt like a child's game of dress-up. Fun and exciting.

Eventually, having the same polite conversations with the same people three times a month got old, and I came to dread them unless I'd had a hand in the event. The planning and execution process allowed me a buffer, a degree of separation from the guests.

Tonight would probably be worse than tedious. Winston was right. I didn't belong there.

And yet, Winston could bite me. I was here to help him, so I tucked my hand through Drew's arm and swung through the doors with barely a moment's hesitation.

"Everly Hastings. You are the very last person I

expected to see here tonight. I heard you'd run off to join the circus or something."

"Hello, Lenore."

It would be my luck to run into the snob queen of the society circuit before my feet made the transition from carpeted foyer to the parquet of the banquet room.

A lifetime of caloric deprivation hadn't kept Lenore Cavendish from aging, nor did the way the light teased a burgundy sheen out of her artificially darkened, used-to-be brunette hair. Nose in the air, dress hanging off her scarecrow-thin frame, she spread joy and sunshine wherever she went ... NOT.

"I'd like you to meet Andrew Parker, who has kindly agreed to be my plus-one for the evening. Lenore has been supporting the arts in our area ever since ... well, long before we were born."

Because Paul had asked it of me, I'd let Lenore get her little digs in at every opportunity, but his opinion no longer mattered, and those days were over. "If you'll excuse me, I see someone else I'd rather talk to."

"Meow," Drew whispered in my ear.

"I edited myself," I assured him.

Drew snorted.

"I did," I said. "If I hadn't, I might have mentioned the fact that if she had one more facelift, her ears would meet in the back." Drew coughed to cover a laugh.

"Do you know she had the nerve to show up at an event to help the homeless I was running and squawk about how she'd give money because it looked good on her tax return, but the bums really should do something to help themselves? She's a heartless snob, and from the back, she looks like a frog walking on two legs."

"That is the most accurate observation I've heard all night." Patrea had come up behind us. "Some wild stories are going around about Winston. He's become sinner to Paul's saint."

"What does that make me? Jezebel?"

"With this one on your arm, absolutely." Patrea watched the crowd shrewdly. "Emily Ballentine is here, and I can almost guarantee she called Tippy Hastings the minute she saw you here with a date. Speaking of, I don't believe we've met." She gave Drew a head-to-toe perusal. "Patrea Heard. I'm Everly's attorney, and you are?"

"Drew Parker. I'm Everly's buffer for the night."

The pair of them sized each other up until Patrea

finally nodded and grinned. "Okay, then. Nice to meet you."

"Well, at least you didn't pee on me to mark your territory."

The comment was meant for Patrea, and I'll admit my nerves were already a little frayed, but Drew answered. "I like to consider myself house-trained."

Patrea laughed. I rolled my eyes but allowed a hint of a smile. "Have you seen Honor anywhere? I think I'd better talk to her and sneak out before the last tray of hors d'oeuvres makes the rounds."

Drew laid his hand on my lower back, gave it a gentle rub. "Or you could stay and show them what you're made of."

"What would that be?" I turned to him. "Vinegar and battery acid?" I felt a hint of remorse for being rude to Lenore.

"Maybe, but there's fire and courage in facing the people who didn't stand with you."

The warmth of a blush tickled across my cheeks, and I couldn't look at him anymore, so I turned to Patrea. "Where's Chris?"

"Over there." Patrea gestured toward a group of men who appeared to be in the middle of a heated debate. "Talking sports with the trophy husbands. He's keeping an eye on the door in case Honor decides to leave. She's at the bar—big shock—doing her level best to drink her weight in gin."

"Then I'd better get to her before she passes out in the coat closet again."

"I'd hurry if I were you. If she's blonde and wearing a dress that's shinier than a disco ball, she just went that way," Drew pointed toward the restrooms.

"That'd be her," Patrea affirmed. "I'll stay here and pump Drew for personal information—I mean keep Drew company, so you can catch up with Honor while she's still on her feet."

Fancy-pants venues are required to have fancy-pants restrooms. It's a rule or something. This one had its own sitting room attached with sofas at one end and a bank of lighted makeup mirrors at the other. The toilets were tastefully enclosed in a separate room through a door at the back.

"Men are jerks." In a skin-tight silver beaded number, Honor did look a bit like a disco ball but didn't seem to be as drunk as Patrea thought she was. I didn't have any trouble getting her to talk. Basically,

I said hello, and then she went off like a champagne cork.

"It's like it's hard coded in their DNA to cheat and lie."

I wanted to disagree because I knew some fine men, I just hadn't married one of them. But I needed information, and she needed a sister solidarity moment, so I put on my cranky voice. "Mine slept with my closest friend, and then threw me out of our house like I was the one who did something wrong. What did yours do?"

Okay, maybe I wasn't entirely over what Paul had done because I didn't have to work too hard for the cranky voice.

"He did my neighbor's dog walker, that's what. Barely eighteen, perky boobs, and legs long enough to wrap around him twice."

"Jerk," I said. "Who did your divorce? Someone good, I hope."

Forgetting she held a glass, Honor waved her hand and splashed gin on herself. Maybe she *was* as drunk as Patrea thought she was. "Sure did. I'll be driving around in Andre's Ferrari with the top down this summer. Winston Durham looks harmless, but he's a shark. Best divorce lawyer in town. Or he was."

Maybe I should have hunted down Andre instead of Honor.

"Too bad what happened to him, isn't it? I wonder who killed him."

About a half-inch of gin remained in her glass, and Honor downed that solemnly, then made an air toast.

"To poor, dead Winston. May he litigate his way through the pearly gates."

I'd have chosen a much more fiery climate to wish him into, but Honor didn't need to know that. When pressed, she denied any shady dealings during her divorce but offered up another tidbit.

"Winnie was good with the legal stuff, but I wouldn't trust him to manage my money."

Ping.

Studying her glass as if wondering why it was empty, Honor elaborated but only after a gentle, verbal nudge.

"Consider the source, but Lenore Cavendish told me she let him manage some of her money, and he did some shady things with it, or maybe he lost it all. Or was it Hilly Cartwright? You know what? I can't remember. And that means I need another drink."

Another drink probably wouldn't improve her

memory, but one might improve my mood. Winston hadn't played fast and loose with Honor's prenup, but he might be the reason Paul had to sell his house.

Even before I crossed the room to rejoin Patrea, she caught my eye, and I shook my head to let her know the news wasn't as good as I'd hoped.

I could leave now or sit through four tedious courses followed by speeches and pleas for more money in the hope of mending fences with Lenore. What could be worse?

As soon as I asked myself, my brain began supplying a list. I hadn't reached Drew and Patrea or decided what to do when a hush fell over the room.

My former in-laws had arrived.

Two things happened at once—out of the corner of my eye, I saw Patrea shove Drew in my direction, and my feet failed to respond to my mental order to stop.

These were people who had treated me reasonably well during my marriage, and yet, they were also the people who had raised the kind of man who would cheat, lie, and possibly murder to get what he wanted.

It seemed like the rest of the room took a collective step back and went silent, so whether I moved forward or not, it looked like I did. To leave, I'd have to walk past them, to stay meant a confrontation, or I'd back down and swallow the angry words that burned on my tongue. Either way, I was in for an evening of being the subject of much attention.

Tippy—and how they got Tippy from Madeleine, I'll never know—glared daggers at me, elbowing her husband Thurston in the ribs. The look on his face when he saw me was about what you'd expect on someone who'd just stepped in a steaming dog pile.

I didn't even need to hear Grammie Dupree's voice in my head to decide I would stick around for the rest of the evening. And when I met Tippy's murderous look with a cocked eyebrow and a nod, the rush of confidence that welled up inside me was icing on the cake.

Wisely, Drew stayed back and let me carry on a silent conversation with my former in-laws that let them know I would not run or hide. Not this time. When Tippy's gaze finally dropped, I turned away. The hushed moment turned to a buzz of scandalized whispers when I joined Drew and let him wrap an arm around my waist.

"I take it we're staying."

Walking away from my former family without a

backward glance, I assured him, "Wild horses couldn't drag me out of here."

I filled Patrea in on my conversation with Honor as we circled around the ten tables to look for the place cards with our names on them. When we found ours on the center table, both Drew's and mine sat slightly askew as if someone had placed them hurriedly.

"Everly." Lenore Cartwright burned me with a look as she seated herself to my right. It looked as if I'd be eating my salmon with a side of crow.

"Lenore," I responded. "I'm sorry if I was a little abrupt with you earlier. Coming here tonight wasn't easy for me, and I'm afraid I took out my nerves on you. I'm sure you understand."

According to the nastiest of rumors, Lenore had married beneath her. Translation from snob code— Lenore married for love, and her husband hadn't been wealthy. Maybe that was why she attended functions alone.

"Better than you think."

I might have misjudged her. Perhaps she hated being here as much as I did.

"How difficult it must be to keep a firm grasp on

your decorum and on the coattails of your betters at the same time."

Or not.

I allowed myself the satisfying mental image of slapping the smug smile off her face while injecting honey into my voice. "You do have exquisite taste in fine outerwear."

Tell me, darling, was that imported or domestic weasel you had on earlier?

If I had to play the game to get information out of her, I would play it like a pro.

With Patrea and Chris seated on the other side of Drew, we were five at a table for eight.

Since Lenore always arrived at these functions alone, she'd be paired with another single to make the numbers work. Can't have an odd number at dinner.

Except that, on this night, we would.

"It's a shame about Winston." I nodded to indicate the empty seat on Lenore's other side. Had his place card been left as an oversight, a tribute, or the catalyst to start something up?

I got my answer when the last two people arrived at their seats at about the same time the wait staff delivered our plates.

"Won't this be fun?" Lenore's dry tone grated on my last nerve, but not as much as the sight of my former in-laws standing across the table from me. I caught the look on Patrea's face and figured our thoughts ran along the same lines.

No way would this end well.

Drew caught Thurston's eye, held that contact as he leaned close to speak quietly in my ear. "Still want to fight those wild horses?" As always, his voice had the power to excite and soothe at the same time. It was uncanny.

"Watch me."

He didn't really have to watch me because I didn't have to do anything for the drama to ramp up. Tippy took care of that all by herself.

"I won't sit here with her," she said to Thurston. "Do something."

Patrea pushed back her chair, prepared to stand up, and go into scary lawyer mode, but I caught her eye and shook my head. "Don't." This was my battle to fight or not to fight as the case may be.

"I'm sure Madeleine has spun a story to her friends that put me in the very worst possible light. Now, like the proverbial bad penny, I've popped back up, and she thinks she can make me live up to her lies by goading me into a public display."

The throbbing vein in Tippy's forehead was a pretty good indicator I'd pegged her correctly.

"That," I said, letting my gaze move from Tippy to Thurston and back again, kept my voice perfectly even and low enough not to travel past it's intended target, "will not happen. I have nothing to prove. So, you can sit down and eat your crab cake, Madeleine, or you can leave in a snit. Your call."

Without waiting for a decision, I turned back to Lenore. "As I was saying, it's such a shame about Winston. Did you know him well?"

Under the table, Drew's warm hand grasped the fist I'd kept clenched in my lap during the confrontation. The heat and the strength that flowed from him had my fingers uncurling until they interlocked with his.

There's nothing stronger than a man who knows when to step in front of a woman and when to stand beside her. I knew right then that I would break my no-men rule for him.

Oh, who was I kidding? I already had.

"Well enough to have my own ideas about who killed him." Now, Lenore had my full attention. Amid the clinking of cutlery and the hum of conversation in the room, Tippy and Thurston decided they had somewhere more important to be.

"By all means, Lenore. Don't keep us in suspense." Patrea gestured with a forkful of roasted sweet potato. When she saw me looking at her, she shot me an approving grin.

"I visited Winston's office a week ... no, a week and a half ago, to talk to him about ... a minor legal matter."

Or a major amount of lost money, I thought.

"When I got there—at the appointed time, I might add—he was with another client, and that harpy who works for him told me I'd have to wait. Dreadfully rude."

While she denounced Winston and his staff for lacking any understanding of basic manners, Lenore dug a silver-plated toothpick out of her purse and proceeded to pick a bit of crab from between her teeth. I bit my lip to keep from smiling and encouraged her to elaborate.

"Punctuality," Lenore continued, "is one virtue Winston did not possess. Nor did he observe proper office decorum. The man frittered away a good ten minutes of my time to participate in a shouting match with Paul Hastings."

"With Paul? What were they shouting about?"

"Are you suggesting I'm the type to listen in on private conversations?"

With her ear pressed up against the door ... or a glass if she could find one and there hadn't been a receptionist to see her snooping.

"Of course not, Lenore. You're the soul of discretion." I actually kept a straight face as I said it, too.

"In any case, Paul did most of the shouting, and he threatened to kill Winston on his way out. When I heard the news, I assumed he'd made good on the threat."

Patrea pressed for more details. "Paul actually said he would kill Winston? In those exact words?"

" 'I could kill you for this.' That is what he said, and that is all I know about the subject." And it was the last she'd speak of it.

The rest of the evening dragged by, and in the car on the way home, I felt compelled to defend myself.

"My life is not usually like this, you know." Except maybe it was. Have I not said I was a bad bet in the dating department? Surely Drew had figured that much out for himself by now. "I don't make a habit of attending ritzy functions just so I can yell at people. I'm more of a stay-at-home, Friday-game-night type of person."

Just great, Everly. Way to make yourself sound appealing to the guy you're mysteriously interested in dating. I hadn't examined the reasons why Drew managed to get past my carefully mounted emotional walls so quickly, and now, there probably wasn't a need for it. He hadn't said much since we'd begun the drive home.

And I couldn't seem to shut up.

Finally, I chanced a look at him. "Are you laughing at me?"

"Not at *you*."

"Well, you're clearly not laughing *with* me. I don't think any of this is funny." Heat prickled over my face, the curse of being a redhead. I'd embarrassed myself by losing control of my emotions in public, and wasn't too far from it happening again in private.

Drew took his eyes off the road long enough to look at me. He didn't say anything for the next few miles but pulled off the highway at the rest stop and parked.

Turning in his seat to give me his full attention, he asked, "Why are you so upset?"

"Because I made a fool out of myself." I did not add *in front of you*, but the thought was in my head.

A beat of silence fell between us.

"Look at me." Drew pried my fingers off the purse I clutched on my lap. Gently, he chafed warmth back into them. My neck felt so tight that my back muscles ached from holding so much tension, and I had trouble turning my head. "Everly, please."

He wasn't laughing now. The way the light fell, it cast shadows over half his face, turned the ordinary planes and angles to works of art carved by a deft hand. "Look at me."

Low and deep and sonorous, his voice was hypnotizing. I looked, and my breath caught. I didn't want to want him. I didn't want to want anyone.

Could be a front. Men lie and cheat. I knew that firsthand. Drew might do the same. My inner voice didn't even sound convinced, and I let the misgivings go as quickly as they surfaced.

There was no other sound but the rustling of his coat as he cupped my face and moved closer. I leaned in to close the gap, mingled my breath with his, and sighed into the kiss.

CHAPTER TWENTY-TWO

"You want the good news or the bad news?" Amber yelled from outside the bathroom door instead of sticking her head through, which I appreciated. My morning had disappeared in a blur of phone calls—most of them from Martha in a premature panic over some minor details with the Valentine's Day event.

Once I had Martha as settled as Martha ever got, I called Officer Bassett to fill her in on what I'd learned from Honor and Lenore. She asked a lot of questions and made me repeat the information several times, then we talked a little bit about Albert's case before the call ended.

"Bad news first."

"I swung over to the motel just in time to catch Reva checking out."

Pushing the mascara wand back into the tube, I said, "I asked for the bad news first." Finished with my makeup, I walked back into the bedroom to find Amber hovering over my bed.

"When she pulled out of the parking lot, she turned toward town. I think she's headed back here."

I sighed. "I guess that qualifies. What's the good news?"

"Cold snap's ending. It's a balmy thirty-five degrees already, and temps are expected to climb another four or five degrees this afternoon."

"Did you hear that, Molly? We're having a heat-wave, and that means an extra-long walk today. And by the time we get home, maybe Reva will be out of our lives for good." I knew it wouldn't be that easy, but a girl can hope, right?

That hope sent me to my closet for a warm coat, hat, and mittens, and my fingers fumbled while clipping on Molly's leash. My thumbs might not have been pricking, but my gut knew something wicked was coming my way.

"I'll stand watch. If she shows up, I'll come and find you," Amber promised.

Molly didn't care why we set off down the sidewalk at a brisk pace, she was just happy to stretch her legs after such a long period of cold weather. Muscles bunching under her sleek, chocolate brown coat, and tongue lolling happily to one side, she enjoyed the pure pleasure of the moment. I envied her the ability.

I felt as though I'd been running away from or toward something ever since the day I moved back to town, but never more than at that moment. With an unbroken stretch of sidewalk in front of me, my faithful dog by my side, I settled into the motion, letting my breathing become the metronome for the pace.

Freed from directing my body, my mind cleared, and my focus sharpened as I looked for a pattern in everything that had happened since the moment my world shattered.

Paul and Reva. Paul and Winston. Both combinations spelled betrayal, and both had Paul in common, so I put him at the center of a widening circle of events and tried to find a path that would lead to Winston's death, Paul missing, and Reva in Mooselick River.

In retrospect, I'd been blinded by the fairytale romance of being swept off my feet by the handsome prince. But all castles double as fortresses, and stone walls can enclose as well as protect.

Under the guise of protection, Paul could easily have been setting me up from the beginning.

Pilfering money from the foundation's coffers for ... well, that detail was hazy since he had plenty of money of his own. Probably needed it to support Reva in style.

When the burn of anger threatened to cloud my thoughts, I forced it back down, listened to the rhythm of my feet on the sidewalk until my emotions settled, then went back to dispassionately contemplating Paul's crimes. I meant to lay out my thinking to Jody Bassett and the detective whose name I could never remember, and let them figure out who killed Winston.

As far as ghosts went, he'd been a relatively low-key annoyance, and as long as someone solved his murder, he could go into the light. I figured I'd do my part by cooperating fully with Basset and company— let them do the legwork on this one.

To that end, I went back to thinking through the timeline of events. If not for a suspicious investor, I might still be living a lie. I owed that guy a basket of muffins or something. Or maybe not, since those suspicions had caused Paul to spring into action and come up with a plan to make me the scapegoat.

It all fit. The prenuptial forgery—unnecessary for any other reason than to make me look desperate—

the staged discovery of his betrayal. He underestimated me there. Assumed I wouldn't question the agreement or remember enough about it to notice the subtle changes. He certainly hadn't counted on Patrea and her handwriting expert.

With me cleared, or mostly cleared, of suspicion in the misappropriation of funds, someone else would have to take the blame. Enter Winston.

Who better to point the finger at than the attorney/finance manager with a reputation for losing people's money? The frame job wouldn't be that difficult. All Paul had to do was forge a few documents to prove Winston had access to foundation funds, and bam! Instant scapegoat.

Take it a step further and kill Winston so he can't prove his innocence, and the case was locked.

And that's where the theory began to break down. The place and time of Winston's death made absolutely no sense in the narrative. Staging the death to look like suicide, complete with a note confessing to the crime, would have put Paul in the clear. Shooting Winston in his own storage room might even have worked. Paul could have claimed he came upon a theft in progress. There'd been a scuffle, and in the middle of protecting his property, the gun went off.

An entirely plausible story if Paul had stuck around to tell it. Why didn't he?

Where would Paul go if he'd done something too horrible to face?

These were questions I should have had enough information to answer. I had spent several years with the man, but with evidence mounting against him, I didn't think I'd known my husband at all.

At about the same time I reached that epically unhelpful conclusion, Amber popped up in front of me. "Am I good, or what? Nailed that prediction perfectly. Reva showed up at your place."

"Is she still there? I've had a minute to think things over, and I have questions she might be able to answer." I turned Molly and headed back toward home with Amber zipping along beside me.

"She's there. Or she was a few seconds ago. Banging on the door, ringing the doorbell, yelling for you to come out because she knows you're in there. It's quite a scene. I expect someone will call the cops if she keeps it up."

Molly needed no urging to step up her pace when I increased mine to a jog. We'd gone a fair distance while I settled on a theory of the crime, and I hoped she'd still be there when I got back.

The one time I actually wanted to see her, she was gone. Talk about Murphy's luck.

To compensate for the abbreviated walk, I played ball with Molly off the back porch until she was done, and followed up with one of her other favorite activities.

All girl, Molly loved a good blow-out. She stood patiently while I toweled off most of the melting snow, and did her happy wiggle when I plugged in the blow dryer.

Finally, dry and happy, she circled several times and settled down on her bed for a well-earned nap while I headed to the kitchen to throw some veggies and broth in a pot.

I'd lost track of time when I heard the front door open and close.

"I'm finished over on Tulip." Comfortable in my house as if he were family, David Barrington walked into my kitchen and helped himself to a glass of water. "I added two inches of rigid foam, sealed up a few air gaps in the foundation, and installed a sensor with an alarm that will go off if the temps near the pipes dip below freezing. It shouldn't be a problem again, but if it is, we'll know ahead of time."

"Fantastic. There's vegetable soup on the stove if you're hungry. Or I can just cut you a check for the work right now." Since the man never turned down food, I went back to what I'd been doing when he arrived.

Instead of pulling a bowl out of the cabinet, David hunkered down next to me. "What are you doing?"

It was a valid question, I supposed. "I'm looking under the stove." Since I had the side of my face pressed to the floor and a flashlight in my hand, the answer should have been self-explanatory.

"I can see that; did you lose something?"

"Misplaced is more like it. I've torn the entire downstairs apart, and now I'm reduced to looking in the more unlikely places." The envelope from Albert was still missing, but I had turned up the notebook from the tower room where Catherine had liked to sit with her camera.

"For?" David prompted.

"An envelope I had the day I moved in. Mom said she left it on the kitchen counter, but it's gone, and I've searched everywhere."

Including behind the refrigerator, and now, under the range. "I'm running out of places to look." While I got back to my feet, I noticed David had gone quiet, and when I looked at him, he had a funny expression on his face.

"I'm sorry." Pushing off from where he'd been leaning against the counter, he walked past me to the free-standing Hoosier cabinet on the opposite side of the kitchen.

"This is all my fault." He reached up and felt behind the arched trim that ran across the top. "I didn't know it was important." When his fingers found what they'd been searching for, he pulled out the envelope. It had several keys scattered on it.

"You remember we were sorting through all those keys on the first day? There were a few that I knew didn't go to anything, and I just used the envelope and stashed them up there out of the way. I intended to go back and get them later, but it was a busy time, and I forgot. I'm sorry, Ev."

All that mattered was I had the envelope now. "Hey." I waved away the apology. "Just goes to show I should have cleaned up there since I moved in. This isn't your fault, and at least I have it now."

"Is it important?"

"Maybe." I wasn't going to open it with him here.

"I'll open it later and find out. Now, Mom told me you stopped in to talk to Martha about properties on the town books, and you're considering pulling an Everly. My folks will be thrilled if you decide to stay in Mooselick River, and I hate to admit it, but you've grown on me, Barrington."

"Pulling an Everly, huh? Not quite. You lucked out buying this place. Catherine kept the place in great condition, but she was one of a kind."

The banter distracted him from asking more questions about the envelope.

"That she was. Is Martha pushing you toward a particular property?"

David pulled out bowls, served us both, and took a seat at the table while I washed up.

"Oh, she's got something in mind." There was both humor and exasperation in his tone. "She thinks I should buy the Marlow."

"The Marlow? I didn't know it was even up for bids. What would you do with an abandoned inn?"

I couldn't picture David as an innkeeper, but I half hoped he'd buy it just so I could get a look inside the place.

"Restore it to its former glory and sell it. I

prowled around the outside, and the structure looks solid, but I'm not buying it without a thorough inspection of the interior. Maybe you could use your connections with Martha to get me the keys."

"Done. But only if you let me go with you when you look at it. I'm dying to see the inside."

With the deal struck, we chit-chatted our way through lunch, then David rinsed his bowl and put it in the dishwasher.

As soon as the door clicked shut behind him, I grabbed the envelope, dumping keys all over the table, and opened the flap. Then I stopped, realized it was the weekend, and shot off a text to Patrea.

—Where are you?

She and Chris were still hot and heavy despite her dire prediction otherwise, and since he had time on his hands until spring planting, they alternated between his place and hers. I didn't think that arrangement would last forever, but for now, they made it work.

Instead of messaging me back, she called. "I'm at the farm, why?" Or I thought that's what she said because the connection was horrible.

"You're breaking up. If you can hear me, I found

the envelope from Albert. Do you want me to open it or wait for you?"

I caught about half of what she said, but it sounded like she would be at my place in fifteen minutes. I could wait that long.

"Amber. Are you around?"

Dead silence. I felt like an idiot and wished I'd asked Kat for a little more practical advice. "Amber. Hell-ooo."

"Keep your pants on. I can hear you, it just takes me a minute to gather myself together."

I made a mental note to ask more about that later, but for now, I didn't want to say anything that would force her to leave.

"Look what I found." I held up the envelope. "Well, David found it, to be honest."

"What's in it?" Amber crowded close enough to send shivers over my body. "I'm dying to know."

"I didn't look yet. Patrea's on her way, but I wanted you to be here, too. Just stay out of our personal space, okay? I'll make sure you can see, and remember, I can't answer questions while Patrea's here."

The way Amber pouted, you'd have thought I'd told her she had body odor or something. "She already thinks the house is haunted, so you could just do us both a favor and tell her about me."

"You sound like a jealous mistress," I said. "What would happen if I did? Huh? Can you show yourself to her?"

Spencer Charles, my second ghost, had made contact with Jacy, but that had been a matter of life and death, and he didn't tell me how he'd done it. Maybe I should have asked, but at the time, I'd been a little busy catching his killer.

Amber sighed. "Probably not. You're easy, but if I had that kind of energy, I'd use it to contact my dad."

CHAPTER TWENTY-THREE

Amber tried to distract me by chattering inanely about the personal lives of people she'd worked with, but the fifteen minutes I waited for Patrea felt more like an hour. But I resisted the temptation to peek at the envelope's contents until she walked through the door, tossed her coat over the newel post at the bottom of the stairs, and kicked off her boots to keep from tracking snow through the house.

"Before we open this bad boy up," I said while she shed her layers and made her way to the kitchen, "I talked to that cop today, the one who's working Albert's case and Winston's murder, and I have some tidbits to share."

At home in my kitchen, Patrea poured herself a glass of iced tea. "Did you mention the argument?"

"I did. And then she asked if he owned a Ruger LCP. That's a handgun, by the way."

"Sure. LCP stands for Lightweight Compact

Pistol. Easy to handle, small enough to tuck into a purse, perfect for concealed carry."

For a moment, I couldn't do anything but stare at her.

"What? I can't know about guns?"

"No, I just ... anyway. To my knowledge, Paul has never even fired a gun, so I said no, and then she asked if I could think of anywhere he might go. They've already checked all the family properties, including the camp on the lake, which is only accessible this time of year by snowmobile. I don't think I was much help because I couldn't think of any place they hadn't already looked. But she did let it slip that he hasn't used his credit or debit cards since he checked out of the hotel."

Arching a brow, Patrea asked, "Does he carry a lot of cash?"

"Bassett asked me the same question, and he didn't carry cash when we were married. Who knows what he does now. While she had me on the phone, she also asked if we owned a metal baseball bat at the time of Albert's attack."

If we had, I might have used it on Paul the day I found him in bed with Reva. In retrospect, I was glad that answer was also a no. Otherwise, I'd probably still be in jail.

"And finally, she pressed me more about my thoughts on the video footage from that day. I stood firm that I didn't think it was Paul, and not just because of the bat. The clothes were all wrong, too."

While Amber hover-paced, Patrea played devil's advocate. "He could have bought a bat and the clothes."

"I suppose you're right. I can't help thinking whatever's in the envelope has something to do with the attack, and that makes me feel horrible."

"You didn't ask for Albert to slip you information. That was a choice he made on his own."

"Thanks for trying to make me feel better, but I won't until he's out of the hospital, and someone is in jail. I really hope there's something in here that can help make that happen." I picked up the envelope.

"Where was it?"

I gestured toward the top of the Hoosier cabinet. "Up there ... and yes, I know you probably clean the tops of your cabinets once a month."

Patrea ignored the comment. "What are you waiting for?"

"Nothing, I guess." I peeled back the flap and

pulled out a sheaf of photos printed in black and white on plain paper.

"From that angle, it looks like it was taken by a security camera." Amber perused the top image. Patrea echoed the sentiment.

"This is security footage. You recognize the office? Is it yours?"

There was no under-watered plant on the desk, so the answer to the last question was no. "It's not mine. Look at the windows ... the view, I mean. That's Paul's office in the corporate building."

Getting a little too close, Amber sent a shiver over me when she pointed. "Look at the time/date stamp."

Patrea moved the first photo over and started a new pile. The second was another still shot of the empty office, and from the same angle, only the time stamps proved we were looking at a series taken on the same night. As we ran through the progression, the office door opened, showed a cleaning cart in the hallway, and finally, a member of the cleaning staff going about her job.

I looked at Patrea, and she looked at me, her baffled expression mirroring my own.

"Is this supposed to be something?" she said.

"Doesn't look like anything out of the ordinary to me."

Amber had a different opinion. "Oh, it's something all right. Look closer at the woman doing the cleaning. Doesn't she look familiar to you at all?"

When Patrea slid that sheet away to reveal the next image, I thought she did.

And so did she. "Is that …? No, it can't be."

"It is, isn't it?"

Minus makeup, wearing a custodial uniform, her hair in a wild tangle of curls, Reva McKinnon apparently had no idea she was on camera as she closed the office door and went to work. The slant of the camera gave us a decent view as she pulled a pin from her hair, and used it on the desk lock.

The timestamp said it took less than two minutes before the drawer popped open. The next image showed her opening the file cabinet with the key she undoubtedly took from the desk drawer.

We kept flipping and flipping. Watched Reva go back to her cart and return with a folder. Watched her scrawl Paul's name on some papers and substitute them for the ones in the file cabinet. Watched her make the office look the way she'd found it.

The real shocker, though, was the final image. It

was taken from the front of the building as Reva got into a waiting car and exchanged a passionate kiss with the driver who was ...

Wait for it ...

None other than Winston Durham.

"Oh no, she did not just do that." Amber voiced my reaction perfectly, but the look on Patrea's face was even better.

"Ew," was all she said before she leafed through the images to get back to the one with the documents.

"Do you have a magnifying glass?"

I did. Or rather, Catherine the Queen of Hoarding did. I got it from the desk and handed it to her.

"I can't make anything out. The text is completely blurred." Patrea set the magnifying glass back down, drummed her fingers on the table. "She forged something, and while all of this is damning evidence, without the document itself, probably not enough for a conviction."

"Well, that's that, then." I gathered the images into a pile and grabbed the envelope to stuff them back in, my movements sharp with frustration.

Something rattled across the bottom.

Eyes wide, I tipped up the envelope and out slide a tiny thumb drive.

"Albert. You wily rascal." Patrea seized the drive, waved it around. "Where's your laptop?"

I was already headed for the bedroom to get it. I flipped the lid and hit the wake-up button on my way back to the kitchen.

Patrea plugged in the drive.

"Wah, wah, wah," Amber intoned when a password protection box appeared.

The celebration over, my mood fell into the basement.

"He meant this for you." Patrea typed my first name into the box. Then my first and last. Then tried again with combinations of capital and lowercase letters. "Okay, that's a no-go."

"Try Alicia," I said, but the results were the same.

We spent a good half hour using combinations of her name and my name. His name and her name. Numbers, symbols. Nothing worked.

"Think about Albert. What do you know about him outside work? Or at work. Does he have a car he loves or a pet? Did you share any little jokes together? It has to be something meaningful to you."

"Or else he intended to tell you the password later," Amber said.

"775 reading 782 math." In my excitement, I spoke louder than necessary. Patrea winced.

"Try it. I know that's it." I said.

On the third combo of spaces and capital letters, we hit pay dirt.

I didn't even notice the chill from Amber crowding in to watch Patrea scroll through the documents.

"Ding, ding, ding. I think we just found ourselves some evidence. Let me send myself a copy of these files, and tomorrow, I'll show them to someone I trust who can tell us exactly what we're looking at. I'd like to make sure both you and Albert are protected when all of this comes to light. In the meantime, put this envelope away somewhere safe."

I did as she requested and put it right back where David had found it. It had been safe enough up there for months—one more day shouldn't matter.

Patrea hadn't been gone a half-hour when my phone played the alert for the camera on the back porch. On the way back there to check, I tapped the notification to bring up the video feed. Nothing there.

Just as expected, but as soon as I headed in that direction, Molly decided she needed to go out.

"You're on your own this time, girl. We'll play ball later." She shot past me, and as the door clicked shut, I heard the unmistakable sound of my front door opening.

"Hello, Everly. We really need to talk."

My pulse ramped up to high speed, and I did the only thing I had time to do, tapped 9-1-1, and hit send. As I turned to face Reva and the gun in her hand, I slipped my phone into my pocket and hoped help would come in time.

CHAPTER TWENTY-FOUR

ithout warning, Reva reared back, swung the gun in an arc that landed hard on my temple. My ears ringing, I went down, and for good measure, she delivered a kick to my side. Pain flared hot and bright, and wet warmth trickled toward my cheek.

"Not so high and mighty now, are you, Everly?" Reva snarled, but I only saw the barrel of the gun staring me in the face. Her voice went in and out, keeping time with the throbbing where she'd clocked me on the temple.

Concussion, I thought. Probably mild, and not helped at all by Amber shrieking profanities at the top of her astral lungs. I wanted to beg her to be quiet, but I didn't dare. Undirected, her fury vibrated through the house, but without enough force to be helpful. Even thrusting her arm through Reva's head had no effect. It shouldn't have come as a shock to me that Reva was insensitive to ghostly energy.

There would be no ghost bowling today. No handy mannequin head to save the day. With Molly penned in the backyard, there was only me. Unarmed and, if not quite alone, pretty close.

"You underestimated me just like that idiot you married. He's lousy in bed, don't you think? Come on, you can say it. We'll keep it just between us girls. Absolutely no imagination whatsoever, that one."

"He did sleep with you, so I suppose you're right." Like an idiot, I earned myself another kick in the side. While she talked about my ex, I ordered myself to breathe through the pain, to use it to sharpen my resolve.

"Is that a Ruger LCP?"

The gun wavered. "This old thing? Sure."

"It's the gun you used to murder Winston." Not a question. I didn't need to ask, only to have her confirm what I already knew. "And it was you who beat Albert nearly to death."

"Now you see, I felt a little bit bad about that one. If he hadn't changed shifts with someone at the wrong time, he wouldn't have recognized me from my night job. I haven't decided what to do with him."

"Leave Albert alone. He can't remember anything

about the attack, and he has a daughter who'll be going to college next year. Kill me if you must, but don't hurt him."

Reva frowned. "I'm not an animal. I don't actually like killing people." Her tone turned conversational. "This is all your fault, you know. If you'd just have taken the blame and gone to jail like I wanted, everyone would have lived happily ever after."

"Everyone?"

"Well, everyone who counts. And by that, I mean me. I had the perfect plan. I was going to marry Paul."

"Didn't you say he was bad in bed?"

Reva laughed again. "Sure, but he does have millions of other attractive attributes."

I shook my head in disgust, then regretted it when the pain pounded through my skull. "Brains isn't one of them."

"You can tell him what you think of him when you see him again."

For a moment, hope flared. Maybe she didn't mean to kill me.

"I'll give you a few minutes for a happy little reunion. It's the least I can do since we were all such good friends. If he's still among the living."

"Where is Paul?" I'd fallen on my phone. Probably not hard enough to break it, but I had no idea if Ernie—or anyone else—had picked up, or could hear. On the off chance, I figured it was best to get as much information out there as I could. "What have you done to him?"

"Oh, he's all tied up at the moment." She laughed at what I assumed was an attempt at a bad pun. "I gave him a little cocktail to keep him nice and quiet and put the Do Not Disturb sign out so he could sleep. Paul hasn't been feeling too well the past few days. Why, I think he might even kill you for what he thinks you did to Winston. But we both know Paul is a bit of a wuss."

The woman was mad. Utterly mad.

She trilled out a laugh. "He won't be able to live with himself, but there's always that nice bottle of pills the doctor prescribed to help calm his nerves."

I used to make fun of the way bad guys in movies always felt the need to unburden their souls at the crucial moment, but I didn't anymore. It's a thing.

"Now," Reva barked. "Get up!"

When I didn't immediately comply, she kicked me again, the pointy toe of her boot jamming into my ribs. "On your feet. Now!"

There were two of her, then one, then two again, and my stomach did a slow roll as I struggled to stand. She waved the gun toward the door. "Get your coat, take your purse. We're going for a little ride."

She might hesitate to fire that gun in here where the neighbors lived close enough to hear it, but if I got in the car with her, I was dead.

Panic threatened to paralyze me until I heard Grammie Dupree's voice in my head.

What are you waiting for, girl? Christmas?

Riley would be annoyed if I didn't use her training.

Push the heel of your hand against the barrel. If you control the head, you control the body. Do whatever it takes to disarm and contain your opponent. Say no. Say it loud. Take back your power. Don't hold back.

It was now or never. I could do this.

"I'll shoot you right here." Reva's sneer lit the fuse, and I went off.

My mind emptied out of everything except for the need to survive. Even Amber's voice faded to silence. Adrenaline fired my blood, washed away all pain and fear, leaving my head crystal clear. I rose up on the balls of my feet, and let the motion carry me forward.

"No!" I shouted and rammed the heel of my hand into the barrel of the gun. Just like Riley had shown us, the pistol slid back, wrecked Reva's grasp, and flew out of her hand.

"Nice one." Amber zipped back and forth through the hallway.

I had a split second to enjoy the surprised look on her face before I grabbed her head and bore her body to the hardwood floor.

"Get off me!" She thrashed her legs around until the hotel keycard fell out of her pocket. I grabbed it, leaned over, and secured her arm against her side like Drew had taught in class. In that position, she couldn't get enough purchase to dislodge me. But then, I couldn't get to my phone to see if my call had gone through, so we were in a stand-off.

"Bite me, Reva." Just because it felt good, I put a little more weight on the knee pinning her head to the floor than was strictly necessary and looked for the gun. With the adrenaline ebbing, Ernie's siren blaring its way toward me was the most welcome sound I'd heard in a long time.

That he banged the door against Reva's head when he rushed in was just icing on the cupcake of my day.

"You came." Ernie and I might have had a bump or two in the past, but I'd never been so glad to see his stolid face before. "How much did you hear?"

"Enough to know she murdered that lawyer fellow. After that, I lost the call." Motioning me back, Ernie placed Reva under arrest. Once he had her hands secured behind her back, he looked me over. "You're bleeding." Moving closer, he assessed the lump on my head. "Probably ought to get that looked at."

"She's crazy," Reva sounded completely earnest, but I knew her well enough to see the crazy behind her eyes. "She held me at gunpoint and made me say all those things. You have no proof of anything."

For a split second, Ernie looked like he might be experiencing a bit of doubt.

"The gun is over there," I pointed to where it had landed. "You heard her say it was the one she used to kill Winston?"

Ernie nodded, and he didn't look doubtful anymore.

"You'll find her fingerprints on the trigger and my palm print—if there is such a thing—on the end of the barrel. It got there when I shoved it out of her hand. Go talk to Riley Parker if you want to know how that worked. In the meantime, there's an envelope on top of the cabinet in my kitchen with all the proof you need that she and Winston were behind the misappropriation of funds that she tried to frame me for."

That nugget of information made Reva flinch.

"That's right," I called her a name that would have made my Grammie Dupree stand up and cheer. "Albert did more than recognize your face." I turned to Ernie. "You'll want to call the feds, but I'm surprised they didn't show up when you did. They're probably watching the house right now."

"No, they aren't. They'd have to tell me if they were. Interdepartmental cooperation and all."

"The white van in the parking lot of the church. It's been there just about every night and morning for a week."

"Belongs to one of Bess Tate's brood of grandkids. He's been painting the church on nights and weekends."

I directed a look at Amber.

"Sorry," she said. "My mistake."

"Fine. Call them then. But right now, there's something I need to do." I had to go find Paul.

Felt convicted to, for some stupid reason.

I grabbed my purse off the table and didn't even bother with a coat. My head still pounded, but I could dry swallow a couple of painkillers along the way.

"You can't leave. You have to make a statement."

Halfway out the door, I turned back. "I'll come to the station and do that as soon as I'm done. Just let my dog in, and lock up after you take out the trash."

"I'm coming with you," Amber said.

Great. Just what I needed.

"Where did you learn that move? I didn't know you could do that." For the first time since I'd met her, Amber wasn't giving me crap about being stodgy or boring. "The look on her face ... I'll never forget it."

"Self-defense courses," I muttered and fished two foil packets of painkillers out of my purse. Because I was driving and needed at least one hand, I used my teeth to rip off the top and then turned my head to spit it out. The movement proved how much I needed the pills.

I had the headache down to a dull roar by the time I hit the off-ramp, but I still winced when I got out of the car.

"Why didn't you just send the cops?" Amber followed me into the elevator.

"I don't know." I gave her total honesty as I fingered the keycard in my pocket. The hotel name wasn't printed on the card, but I'd recognized it by the deep blue with a white stripe across the front. Was it irony or just plain karma for Paul to be held captive in his favorite suite?

Or maybe not. The door remained stubbornly locked.

"I'm glad you're here." Those were words I never thought I'd say to Amber. "Can you poke your head in and see if he's in there?"

She took me at my word and literally poked her head in, then withdrew it quickly.

"Uh, nope. Not unless he's suddenly aged about forty years and has taken an interest in cosplay."

I so did not want to know.

"Okay, what do I do now? The numbers aren't marked on the room keys. Some sort of anti-theft thing, I'm sure, but I can't try it in multiple doors for the same reason. Too many tries in the wrong door triggers security measures."

"Aren't you glad I came along? And that I didn't go into the light?" Amber preened. "I'll just zip through and find him for you. Maybe you should spend that time thinking about what kind of reward you'd like to give me."

"I still can't afford to take you to Paris."

"You're no fun."

"Just do it, please."

With a cheeky grin, Amber zipped to the end of the hall and stepped through the door while I tried to ignore the invasion of privacy I'd just initiated.

She wasn't gone for more than a minute.

"He's not on this floor. Are you sure we're in the right hotel?"

"I'm sure."

"Okay, wait here."

She was gone longer this time. Long enough that I felt like a creeper hanging out in the hallway, so I found the alcove with the vending machines and waited there until she called my name.

"He's two floors up. Third room on the left."

"Alive?"

Amber nodded, her eyes dancing, but refused to elaborate. I didn't push her as I readied myself to face Paul after all this time. The elevator ride seemed to take forever and was over all too quickly. Stopping in front of the third door on the left, I sucked in a deep breath, winced when my ribs hurt, and let the pain remind me of everything I'd been put through either directly or indirectly by this man.

"I'll just stay out here," Amber said.

My fingers trembled, but I slid the card into the slot and watched the light turn green.

CHAPTER TWENTY-FIVE

*P*aul wasn't dead. He wasn't drugged and sleeping, either. What he was, was naked.

Naked, gagged, and chained to the bed.

I'm proud of myself for not succumbing to the temptation to make this a Kodak moment.

His eyes went wide when he saw me, then went frantic when he realized I'd come to set him free.

Keeping my eyes averted, I threw a blanket over him.

"Can you tip your head forward a little so I can unhook this?" She'd used a ball gag that buckled in the back.

"Everly. Thank God," he rasped. "Reva—"

"Don't. I already know." I left him long enough to fill a glass with water, tipped it up so he could drink. "The police have her in custody for the murder of Winston Durham, the attempted murder of Albert

Runyon, and a host of other charges to do with the theft of funds from your family's foundation."

"I'm sorry."

"As well you should be." Looking at the man I'd stood in front of friends and family and vowed to love forever, I felt...surprisingly little. Pity for him being so easily duped. A touch of nostalgia, maybe, but nothing of anger or longing or even pain. There was something else, though, but before I had time to explore my emotions more deeply, he spoke again.

"I messed everything up." His voice sounded stronger now. "It was all Reva's fault. She got into my head. Convinced me you were a gold digger who only married me for the money."

"Is that so?" I kept my voice light as I looked at the system of chains Reva had used to keep Paul trapped. "Well, you're free of me now, aren't you? No more worries on that score."

Padlocks secured shackles to his wrists and ankles.

"Is the key here? I hope she didn't have it with her, or we'll have to call in someone to cut these chains. Or maybe a locksmith. I'm not sure."

"Look at me," Paul pleaded.

"I am looking at you. And I know you've been

through a lot. Help me help you. Tell me where to find the key."

"I'm trying to tell you I still love you."

At that moment, I figured out the other emotion I'd been feeling. I tipped back my head and laughed even though it made my ribs ache. Paul, however, was not amused.

"Saying I love you should mean something. I don't understand why that's so funny."

"I agree." Since he wasn't helpful, I scanned the room for the most likely place Reva would put the key, and found it hanging in plain sight on the back of the door. "Ah, there we are."

Snagging the ring off the hook on the door, I went back to him, unlocking his ankles first, then his wrists. When he reached for me, I threw the key on the bed and stepped back.

"No, Paul. I said I agreed that saying I love you should mean something, and to me, it does. So when I tell you that I don't love you, you should know that means something, too."

He rubbed at the red places on his wrists then reached for me again. "I know I hurt you, and I don't blame you for wanting to hurt me back, but we can move past this, right? You'll come home where you belong, and we'll be us again."

"There is no us. I'm not sure there ever was. I came here to set you free, and I've done that in more ways than you could ever imagine. If I were a different type of woman, I could have used this situation to get something from you, or for revenge. Just think how it would have played on the news. You in all your glory trussed up like a Thanksgiving turkey. I've spared you that embarrassment, and now I'll spare you more."

Looking him straight in the eye, I spoke from my heart.

"I am over you, but here's a piece of advice. Do better, Paul. Try harder. If you want to be with someone who wants you for more than what's in your pockets, then you need to *be* more than what's in your pockets. Do you understand?"

He nodded, and I walked away.

Free.

It felt amazing.

Everly thought she was finally catching her breath after

all the chaos—but in Mooselick River, trouble has a way of finding her.

Keep reading for a preview of the next book, Fortune Haunter, where Everly discovers that some secrets are worth their weight in gold—and some are deadly enough to bury you.

~Also Available in Audiobook & Paperback Versions~

There's also a novella that can be read as a standalone, but fits chronologically between this book and *Fortune Haunter*. It's called Teen Spirit, and you can get it on Amazon or read it for FREE with your Kindle Unlimited subscription.

Quick Author's Note

If you've made it this far, thanks for spending some time in Everly's world! We're ReGina and Erin, the mother-daughter team behind the *Haunted Everly After* series. Writing together means plenty of brainstorming, lots of laughs, and the occasional heated debate over whether Everly's antics have gone too far. (Spoiler alert: they never do.)

Growing up in rural Maine has given us endless inspiration for our fictional town of Mooselick River. The winding backroads, local legends, and colorful characters are all part of what makes small-town life so special—and just a little bit spooky.

Next up? In Fortune Haunter, a local fortune hunter's death raises more questions than answers, Everly's family is drawn into a search for hidden treasure, and Everly finds herself tracking down a killer. Because in Mooselick River, some fortunes are best left unfound... and some secrets refuse to stay buried.

Anyway, if you've come this far with us and not decided we're complete and total whackadoodles... and especially if you have, we're offering a chance to sign up for our newsletters— the best place to get new release updates, sales notifications, and other fun content.

You can sign up for ReGina's newsletter and/or Erin's newsletter and as a thank-you gift for hanging out with us, you'll also get a FREE novella that isn't available anywhere else. And of course, we promise not to SPAM your inbox!

Love, hugs, and happy reading,
ReGina & Erin

P. S. If you enjoyed this book, it would be great if you could leave a review or recommendation on Amazon, GoodReads, or BookBub.

Your reviews help indie authors sell more books!

I managed to go six whole months without stumbling over a dead body—a personal record for me. A record that shattered like delicate crystal on a fine summer morning. Don't laugh; you probably have your own hurdles in life, and I hope they have nothing to do with the dearly departed.

Unfortunately, mine do.

And that was why my dog, Molly, dropped to her haunches and whined. The sight of a pair of skinny legs sprawled across the rocky trail at the bottom of the slate quarry didn't surprise me as much as it should have done. I knew those legs by the three-inch cuffs and frayed material. Only one man in town wore flannel-lined jeans even in the burgeoning heat of early June.

"That's Delly Harper," I said, and from what I

could see, old Delly wasn't moving. My hand flew up to cover my mouth as I rushed forward to call out, "Are you all right?"

Utter silence but for the distant sound of running water told its own tale.

Not too far from where we stood, a bend of the Mooselick River brought it close to the long-defunct Barrow quarry where Drew had brought me to face my fears after nearly dying there almost a year before. Neither of us expected to find anything other than my lost courage.

"Do you see him?" Distracted, I let go of Molly's leash and clamped my hand on Drew's arm. "He's not moving. I think he's dead."

Of course, he was dead. How could he be anything but dead with his eyes all glazed over and staring directly into the emerging sun? He had to be dead, or else he'd have blinked by now—probably not the most astute of observations, but it's amazing the random thoughts that pop into one's mind during moments of great stress.

Too late, Drew spun me away. "You don't have to look."

"Can't unsee him now." The sight was already burned into my corneas. With shaking hands, I pulled out my cell and checked to see if I had a signal. One bar. Not enough. And wouldn't you know, the only spot in the belly of the pit that had more than two bars was almost on top of the corpse—just my luck.

But even with my feet planted far enough away and leaning over the body, the connection refused to go through the first time. While I waited, I got an uncomfortably close look at the awkward way Delly's head no longer lined up with his body.

"Broken neck," Drew stated the obvious. "Looks like he fell."

My mind helpfully supplied an imaginary movie of Delly sliding over the edge, his arms pinwheeling as he tried to keep his balance. I even heard the faint echo of a startled cry.

A shudder shook me as I tapped 9-1-1 into my phone again. "How sad to die out here alone."

Just saying the word alone sent my guts into knots, but I dismissed the fluttering sensation and waited for the phone to ring on the other end of the line. Finally, it did.

Whether or not the dread settling in the pit of my stomach came from a sixth sense or just from close proximity to yet one more dead body, I couldn't tell.

It wasn't my first time, so I knew better than to disturb anything as I leaned over the body and listened to the phone ringing.

My least favorite dispatcher picked up on the second ring. "What's your emergency?"

"Hey, Carol Ann. I...uh...need to report an accident."

"Ernie," she shrieked loud enough I had to yank my phone away from my ear. "It's that Everly Dupree on the line. Says she needs to report an accident. Probably killed someone again."

"What do you mean *again*?" I heard disdain in her voice and the sucking sound of her straw draining something out of a plastic cup. "Just put Ernie on, okay?"

The next thing I heard was the terse voice of our town lawman. "Polk."

"I did not kill anyone."

A sigh. "You never do, and yet someone's always dead. Who is it this time?"

"Molly," I shouted when Molly's head went up, and she raced out of sight in a blur of sleek chocolate fur and pounding feet.

"Molly who? Have you gone mad?" I could all but hear Ernie yank the phone away from his ear.

I didn't waste time arguing the point. "Sorry, my dog just took off. It's Delly Harper. We found him in the quarry." I pictured our location on a map in my head. "Near where the river bends in toward the pit. Behind the Jackson place."

Ernie and I might not see eye-to-eye on everything, but there were two things I knew about him. One, a little judicious flirting might get a girl out of a ticket, but he was a good cop even when it cost him dearly. And two, he didn't—as a rule—spout profanity on the job. Until today, anyway, but I sensed true grief behind the spate of cussing.

"I told that half-witted fool to put a fence along the edge of that cliff." He swore some more. "Probably got himself half-snockered on cheap wine, went digging for those stupid jars again, and lost his footing."

"Maybe. I'm not getting any closer than I have to, but I don't smell booze on him from here." I went on to describe the condition and approximate location of the body, but the quarry pit wound a fair way and looked very different from below than from above. One path through rocks and bushes looks a lot like any other, and while I had a general idea where we were, I couldn't give exact directions.

"I'll have Drew hike back out to the main road and wait for you. He can show you the way."

Given a choice between dealing with the dog while keeping an eye on the body and getting turned around on a path I hadn't paid enough attention to on the way in seemed like a no-brainer to me.

"Don't touch anything. I'll be there in ten, fifteen at the most." The line clicked dead.

"Like I didn't know that already." At least this time, the death looked to be from natural causes. Still, once the call ended, I put some distance between myself and the body just in case Delly's spirit hadn't gone yet.

"Your hands are shaking," Drew took them in his, stilled most of the trembling with his touch. A deep breath took care of the rest and let me center myself again.

After my marriage ended in a bitter divorce, I hadn't planned on dating anyone. Not ever. Once burned and all that jazz. I hadn't counted on meeting Drew Parker when he opened up a gym in Mooselick River, and it wasn't only his body that sparked a powerful attraction between us right from the first moment.

Drew carries an ineffable air of calm and reassurance—and yes, I realize I've just made him sound boring, but he's not. He's the perfect blend of confident but not cocky. Hot, but not conceited. And if attraction had been all I felt, I could have resisted falling into a relationship. I've worked hard at not being the type of woman to be led around by her hormones.

But there was more to it, to him and to us, than that. It's hard to describe, but being with him made me feel both protected and more resilient—and not only because of the self-protection skills he'd taught me. This morning's quarry hike had been Drew's idea. He thought it would empower me if I faced the fear brought on by nearly dying here. It was the first step, he said, toward us eventually rappelling down the face of the quarry in tandem.

That would not be happening, but he still held out hope. I like that about him.

From not too far away, I heard a short bark and then the unmistakable sound of my dog's paws pounding the ground in the opposite direction she'd left from. One of my favorite things about Molly is that she runs as she does everything else—with great abandon but absolutely no sense of style or grace.

"See, here comes Molly back again. I think we

should wait for her and then you can come with me. There's nothing more to do for Delly, and it's not like he's going anywhere."

A sharp chill that had nothing to do with the damp morning crept over the small clearing and over me. When Drew didn't so much as bat an eyelash, my heart sank. Dead body, creepy chill in the air—all signs pointed to one thing: ghost

And that was why, when Delly shivered into sight behind Drew, I wasn't even a little bit surprised.

Accidental death?

Probably not. Every ghost I'd met so far had been the victim of either out-and-out murder or, in one case, unsolved vehicular manslaughter. I could get lucky and find out Delly had some other type of unfinished business that kept him on the wrong side of the veil, but I wouldn't bet the farm on it.

"No." I sighed, shrugged the backpack straps off my shoulders, and settled down on a flat rock away from the body. "He's not, but it doesn't seem right to just leave him here alone. You go, Molly will stay with me. I'm okay now, and we'll be fine. The faster Ernie gets here, the sooner we can go home."

Delly paced the few steps between his body and the trail, his gaze darting left then right before he locked eyes with me. He picked up on my subtle head-shake, and though he quivered like a nervous chihuahua with the effort, kept silent.

"Go," I repeated. "You'll move faster alone."

"Okay, but stay right here. Don't go off on your own. Take this." Drew pulled a leather-sheathed knife from the side pocket of his hiking shorts. "Just in case."

In case of what, I wondered as he kissed me.

I noted the crestfallen look on Drew's face. "I'm sorry we won't get to finish our empowerment exercise."

Not many men I'd known would have heard a woman utter that phrase without rolling their eyes, but Drew had used it first.

"It's okay. Another time." He kissed me again, then before I could do more than frown at the false note I heard in his tone, he headed back the way we had come, leaving me temporarily alone with Delmar Harper.

Panting with her efforts, Molly arrived before Drew's backpack disappeared from sight. She danced up to me, dropped a piece of moldering red cloth at my feet, and went into a crouch with her hind end up in the air—her *waiting for me to throw the ball* pose.

While I eyed the filthy remains of what I thought might once have been part of the bodice of a dress, Delly spoke.

"She's gonna die if you don't save her."

Fortune Haunter is available now, or if you'd rather save money, you can grab the box set of books 4-6 in the series for a discount. Keep reading for a preview of the free novella you'll get for joining our newsletters.

A FREE STORY FOR YOU

Enjoyed meeting Everly? Not ready for her story
to end?

Sign up for either or both of our newsletters and
you'll receive *A Snowball's Chance in Spell*, a prequel
novella featuring characters from the *Mag & Clara
Balefire Mysteries*, the *Haunted Everly After Mysteries*,
and the *Psychic Seasons* series.

Christmas is canceled! Lexi Balefire's faerie
godmothers didn't mean to knock Santa Claus and
his sleigh out of the sky, but now his reindeer are
missing, and it's up to Lexi to find them all before
time runs out and Christmas is ruined!

Excerpt from A Snowball's Chance in Spell

~

Lightning flirted in shadows of the dark clouds hovering over my house when I came home from work the afternoon before my twenty-second Christmas Eve. Nothing unusual there. With three elemental faeries living in the house, weird weather happened all the time. Or rather, every time my temperamental godmothers mounted some sort of snit.

The godmothers idled at snit.

Going back to work wasn't an option. I'd cleared the last match of the year—a lovely couple with a shared affection for online gaming—and I was no coward. When it came to diffusing faerie fights, I consider myself an expert, and this one didn't look like it rated more than a two on the volcano scale.

Yes, you heard right. I measure faerie fights on the scale of whether or not a volcano might erupt in my backyard. Living with faeries is never boring. Occasionally dangerous—especially because I have yet to come into the magic that is my birthright, but never boring.

A quick check proved they'd contained the madness to the inside and/or the backyard. The two feet of snow on the front lawn was still there and still white—you try explaining black snow to your neighbors sometime. I didn't see any winged denizens—fae or otherwise—dotting the roof ridge, or hear any ominous sounds. If not for the fact that lightning is rare in Maine during the winter, and rarer still when confined to a single area, I'd have thought it was a quiet day in the household.

In my head, I downgraded the threat to a level one, and went inside.

For the most part, my place looks like an ordinary, New England style home. Built by my great grandparents, it's the oldest house in a neighborhood that grew up around it when the suburbs expanded into what was once a rural area. Because, I think, the faeries wanted to give me a normal upbringing, they left the house in mostly the same condition it was in when they came to take care of me and only added on a wing for their own use.

I stepped into the front hall expecting...well, just about anything. Did I mention the faeries love holidays? Maybe they don't have them in the faelands, or maybe they do and go overboard there, too. I can't say since I've never been, but I could tell at a glance there were more decorations than there had been when I left.

"Terra!" I yelled, but got no answer. Terra, faerie of earth, held sway over all the flora and fauna found on dry land. She would be the one responsible for the pine boughs twining over anything that held still long enough. Fire faerie, Soleil, contributed by setting sparks of faerie light to twinkle inside the delicate ice bubbles crafted by her sister, Evian, mistress of water. The effect was lovely, but not as lovely as the three women could be when their faces weren't twisted, as they were now, with rage.

I came upon them in their favorite fighting grounds: the kitchen. It looked like I'd caught this one early since there was relatively little damage done so far. Steam rose from a puddle of water at Soleil's feet which I assumed had come from Evian. Vines snaked from between the kitchen tiles to twine around Evian's ankles, and there were a few smoking embers dotting Terra's hair. Nothing more than a minor spat.

Keeping it casual, I asked, "What's going on?"

There's no rhyme or reason to what will settle a fight or send one into the red zone.

Terra turned one granite pink eye in my direction. "This doesn't concern you." The fingers of her left hand twitched and the vines slithered from Evian's ankles to her knees.

Retaliating, Evian conjured a gush of water from thin air, and doused the smoking embers. The scent of pine boughs couldn't compete with the stench of burnt hair, or the pungent funk erupting from the flowers that burst into bloom near her feet.

"Now look," I pointed out to Terra before she conjured something worse. "Evian is trying to help."

"Was not." Evian snapped her fingers and turned Terra's wet hair white with frost, except because the vines were now questing higher, she overshot the mark and doused a few of Soleil's decorative sparkles.

That was the moment I lost control.

Oh, who am I kidding? I never had control.

Soleil let out a screech and lobbed a fireball at Evian, who encased it in a ball of water and batted it toward Terra. I felt scoured clean when Terra called all the dirt and dust in the house to form a layer over the bobbing ball of doom which now resembled a small planet whizzing back toward Soleil.

It might have ended better if I'd have kept my mouth shut, but I didn't.

"You're going to put an eye out with that thing."

The ire of three faeries is a potent thing, but not as potent as a flaming mudball. I ducked, rolled, and hit the latch on the patio door in what I'd like to think was a graceful move. Probably looked like a seal rolling off a rock.

The flaming fireball arced over my head, its warm breeze tossing my hair, and rocketed off into the sky.

Crisis averted. Except, it wasn't. I should have known.

A Snowball's Chance in Spell is only available by signing up for one of our newsletters here:
https://reginawelling.com
https://erinlynnwrites.com

If you'd like to meet more people who live rent-free in our heads, here's a list of other series we've written. Our books are all set in fictional towns in Maine, and some characters like to flit back and forth between series. The cast of Psychic Seasons hangs out with Everly and also with Lexi Balefire from the Fate Weaver series. Mag and Clara Balefire are Lexi's grandmother and aunt!

Psychic Seasons
Four women, four love stories, and a whole lot of supernatural surprises. In the quaint town of Oakville, Maine, psychic visions, ghostly whispers, and fate itself conspire to change lives—and hearts—forever

Ponderosa Pines Mysteries
Nothing bad ever happens in the weird little town of

Ponderosa Pines...until someone dies. Now it's up to best friends Chloe and EV to solve the mystery—before the town's secrets bury them too.

Fate Weaver

Lexi Balefire—matchmaker, witch, and accidental fate-weaver—must balance love, magic, and a family legacy of chaos before destiny decides for her!

Mag and Clara Balefire Mysteries

Sister witches Mag and Clara Balefire move to a sleepy Maine town for a fresh start—only to find themselves conjuring up trouble, solving murders, and keeping their magic under wraps in this charmingly witchy cozy mystery series

Laurel Haven Witches

Four witches, destined by blood and magic, must embrace their power, battle a dark legacy, and surrender to the love that could break the curse—or bind them to it forever.

Nell Page: Accidental Investigator

Nell Page owns a bookstore, drinks too much coffee,

and has a habit of noticing things she probably shouldn't. With warmth, wit, and an accidental talent for investigating, Nell tackles mysteries that don't always involve murder—but always matter.